SECRET—AT ALL COSTS

The shoulder-fired missile struck the front of the helicopter, breaking off the nose of the Apache and part of the rotor. The aircraft fell like a kid's broken toy.

The chopper hadn't exploded on contact. The pilot tried to free himself from the mangle of metal and heavy Plexiglas. Small-arms fire rattled from the mountainside toward him, followed by enemy soldiers determined to capture the pilot—and his downed helicopter. The pilot wasn't going to let that happen. He reached for the explosives button, fumbling until he worked off the safety guard, waiting until the enemy got closer. He wasn't going alone . . .

EAGLE ATTACK TEAM

LARRY HICKS

DIAMOND BOOKS, NEW YORK

EAGLE ATTACK TEAM

A Diamond Book / published by arrangement with
the author

PRINTING HISTORY
Diamond edition / February 1991

ISBN: 1-55773-459-3

Diamond Books are published by
The Berkley Publishing Group,
200 Madison Avenue, New York, New York 10016.
The name "DIAMOND" and its logo
are trademarks belonging to Charter Communications, Inc.

PRINTED IN THE UNITED STATES OF AMERICA

10   9   8   7   6   5   4   3   2   1

Dedicated to my Kiowa brother,
Clifton Tongkeamah, "Comes from the water,"
Korean War veteran and descendant of the
great Kiowa war chief Sate-Tanta, "White Bear,"
known in history as Satanta.

MEMBERS
OF EAGLE ATTACK TEAM

Lieutenant Colonel Mack "Truck" Grundy, U.S. Army, retired, Korean War and Vietnam War veteran, infantry, Special Forces, parachute, helicopter and fixed-wing qualified.

Chief Warrant Officer 4th Class Cliff "Bad Bear" Sate-Zalebay, U.S. Army, retired, Vietnam War veteran, Special Forces, parachute, helicopter qualified, demolition expert, Kiowa Indian.

Lieutenant Johnny "Crackers" Grahame, U.S. Navy, retired, for minor medical disability, helicopter qualified, test pilot.

Lieutenant Colonel Matty "Red Dog" Bavaros, U.S. Air Force, Vietnam War veteran and Air Force commando in Laos, helicopter and fixed-wing rated.

Commander Charles "Chuck" Taylor, U.S. Navy, Vietnam War veteran, ex-POW and resident of "Hanoi Hilton," flew Jolly Green Giant on rescue in Vietnam.

Major Todd "Jumper" Mason, U.S. Army, Vietnam War veteran, Special Forces, paratrooper and helicopter qualified.

Major Steve "The Gooch" Guccine, U.S. Army, helicopter pilot and Vietnam War veteran.

Command Sergeant Major William "Willie" Falloure, U.S. Army, retired, Special Forces and paratrooper qualified, Vietnam War veteran, covert assignment in Laos with code name of "Black Panther," expert working with indigenous personnel in counter-guerrilla.

Lieutenant Colonel Donald "Bo Peep" Day, U.S. Air Force, retired, Vietnam War and Laos veteran, flew observation planes with Raven Project in Laos, and multi-engine qualified.

Warrant Officer 1st Class Jackson "Push" Okahara, U.S. Army, AH-64 helicopter maintenance specialist, veteran of Panama invasion in 1989.

EAGLE
ATTACK
TEAM

1

Truck Grundy looked at the big, ugly helicopter sitting on its pad. Even under the electric lights he could see the seams of its heavy armor plating, its stubby, cutoff lines making it gawky in appearance. The helicopter sat on three wheels, two in front and a dragger-type tail wheel in the rear. Its stubby "winglets" made it look like an airplane cut short in the wing department. From the winglets hung pods of Hellfire tank-killing missiles and 2.75-inch rockets. In the front end of the helicopter, under its chin, hung an M-230 30mm chain-gun cannon, which looked like a misplaced penis. The craft could carry eight 100-pound Hellfire missiles as well as 1,200 rounds of 30mm ammunition at a speed of 190 knots. Its looks belied its speed and its maneuverability. This helicopter Truck was looking at was the AH-64 Apache, the most rugged, heavily armed, and fastest craft with hard body in the world.

Truck turned to Bad Bear Sate-Zalebay and asked, "You ready to take this bird for a workout?"

"Let's get aboard, boss, and run it through its paces," was the tall Indian's answer. Bad Bear, a retired army chief warrant officer, was Truck's best friend.

Some crewmen ran to assist the two to get in the helicopter and get it ready for takeoff.

Truck got into the front seat, where the gun controls were located, and Bad Bear climbed into the raised backseat, the pilot's seat. Truck had lost an eye in combat and was not able to fly the helicopter at night, for the night-flying device over his right eye made it impossible to see the aircraft's instruments. A man needed two good eyes to fly this craft.

The two men put on their helmets with the night-seeing device attached called TADS/PNVS, standing for target acquisition and designation sight/pilot's night-vision sensor. The device was placed over one eye, making them look like pirates from outer space. Truck did not have an eye patch on his left eye—his was scarred from shrapnel. He could never keep track of eye patches, and always wound up losing them.

"Let's crank her up and go beat up some Texas night air," said Bad Bear over the intercom.

"I hope these cameras work," put in Truck. He wanted pictures of the results from this run.

"I just fly these birds, I don't take pictures," Bad Bear informed him as he hit the switch to crank one engine and then the second one. The two huge General Electric turbine engines spat to a start and steadied down to a roaring whir. He checked all gauges and instruments, waiting for the engines to crank up to their running RPM. When the rotary gained its lift speed, he applied the proper pitch, and the gangly-looking craft sprang off the pad and leaped straight into the air at 500 feet per minute. Bad Bear reached a proper altitude and dropped the nose to get forward movement.

Skimming over the barracks of Fort Hood, Texas, Bad Bear set a course for the target range to which they were assigned. There was plenty of room on this large army post, where tanks and artillery had acres to practice for war.

"Come in from the south, below radar, and let's try to hit our first targets with a Hellfire from behind the trees," ordered Truck.

"Roger, boss," said Bad Bear.

Lieutenant Colonel Truck Grundy, U.S. Army, retired, was one of the best helicopter jockeys in the business. But after he had lost his eye in combat, he had been regulated to running the bush with Special Forces. He was an old hand at the Green Beret business, having earned his Prefix 3 long before they were authorized to wear the beret.

After retirement, he continued to work for the government on covert missions and special projects. As a retired pilot, he usually was not kept out of the cockpit because of a missing eye, but this one was an exception. Although he was an expert at flying the Apache, he was regulated to be a gunner since he could not fly with one eye covered by the TADS/PNVS device.

"Okay, Bear, we're about two klicks from our target," Truck told him. "Got it on the screen. A tank—sitting still. Hellfire. Fire one!" There was a pause, "Just for the hell of it, fire two!"

Bad Bear pushed the stick over to one side and the Apache slipped sideways at about forty-five knots per hour. That was the fastest for any known chopper.

"I have another target. One point six kilometers," called Truck. "Two tanks, one hundred and twenty feet apart." He read his instruments and fired the first and second Hellfires nearly instantaneously.

"At ten hundred hours, six targets! Armored personnel

carriers! Two kilometers. Let's go get 'em, Bear," ordered Truck.

The Apache shot forward, quickly closing on the targets at 190 knots per hour.

Truck could see the APCs in the green glow of the sighting device. He pressed the button and cut loose with the 30mm chain-gun cannon, the cannon swinging in the direction of the movement of his head. A long burst of chain-gun fire poured into one APC, practically disintegrating it piece by piece. Truck fired three rockets at three other targets, and they flew apart as if exploding internally, scattering pieces of armor in all directions. He fired four rockets into a bunker complex, sending broken logs, rocks, and dirt, followed by pieces of sandbags, scattering all to the four winds. In a few minutes, the area was devastated.

The two men flew around the target area, popping off all their load of Hellfire missiles, rockets, and cannon ammunition. There were no misfires.

A good armorer, thought Truck.

"Don't ya wish we'd a had this thing in Nam, Truck?" asked Bad Bear.

"That's an affirmative, 'cause this is one awesome bird. Let's go home," Truck told Bad Bear.

"Got it," was the answer as he set a new course and returned to the army airfield. He flew in to the Apache area and dropped down beside three other AH-64s, landing softly on the hard stand.

Truck took off his helmet and got out of the Apache. He was followed by Bad Bear. Both men wore flight suits with no rank or unit designation.

Truck walked up to a colonel standing with his staff and civilian tech reps. He told the colonel, "I'll take it."

"Two more to go, eh? We'll have them ready tomorrow," the colonel informed him. He wished he knew what they were for, but knowing Truck Grundy, he knew he would never find out. All he knew was that Truck had orders to receive six of the top Apaches in his command. He didn't like to lose them, but Truck Grundy had orders. When Truck Grundy had orders, they were never questioned by a mere colonel.

Truck walked to his car, put on his cowboy hat, and got in. Bad Bear got in on the passenger side and slapped his hat on with an eagle feather stuck in the hat band. Truck drove off.

"Wonder what those two are working on?" asked a major.

"I have no idea, Major. Those two have been together ever since Nam. When they do something, you can bet your last paycheck it's highly classified and dangerous."

The colonel watched the car drive off. He hated to lose six of his Apaches. He went to his own sedan to go home. He had a wife waiting for him.

2

The political stability of the Philippines was deteriorating rapidly. President Corazon "Cory" Aquino was being assaulted from three fronts. Those three fronts were independent of each other, yet all three were trying to topple her administration and the democratic government of the Philippines.

The new vice president was Aquino's most formidable opponent in the opposition. He was a holdover and part of former Filipino strongman Ferdinand Marcos's administration.

In the south, on the islands of Mindanao and Palawan, and the Sulu Archipelago, the Moros were rattling their wavy, double-edged krises. They had set aside their internal differences, and their military arm, the Moro National Liberation Front, the MNLF, was loudly demanding full independence from the central government in Quezon City. These Islamic people were still religious and ideological enemies of the Communists. But government intelligence had uncovered upsetting information that the MNLF was trading military equipment to the Communist New People's Army, better known as the NPA. In return, the NPA was giving control of Mindanao to the Moros.

The Communists were becoming stronger because of the unrest among the poor, who were disappointed by lack of the government's movement to force land reform and impatient for their share in the wealth. This unrest was fueled by the propaganda of the NPA. The NPA was growing and had increased their regulars to more than 50,000 men and women, with supporters and sympathizers numbering as many as 1 million.

NPA strongman Commander Skull had increased his power and was a threat in the north of Luzon. Skull's power had spread from the southern area of the Sierra Madre north to Casiguron on the coast, and to Corlon at the southern end of the Cagauan Valley. His main fort was located in the nearly impenetrable rain-forested mountains of the Quirino Province.

Central committee members of the Communist party of the Philippines–Marxist-Leninist—better known as the Huks—felt that Skull was a threat to their power. His military activities had increased possible presence of the Filipino army, which threatened the existence of the CPP-ML. The NPA was the military arm of the CPP-ML, but the Central Committee of the Party had no control over the many factions within the party. If Commander Skull wished to beat his chest and challenge the Quezon City government, then he had the right and power to do so.

The leaders of the CPP-ML had their own disturbing intelligence about Commander Skull. They had learned that Skull was using money from Filipino drug cartels to finance his military actions and civilian programs. The brutal, but charismatic military leader quoted history in reminding his detractors that the French military had used money from drugs to conduct their war in Indochina in the 1940s and '50s. He laughed about their threat and said he would clear out the drug cartel as soon as he won what was needed for the People's Revolution.

War clouds hung dark and thick over the Philippines, with dour predictions of government failure. Women went to churches and mosques to pray for peace. Military men cleaned and oiled their weapons for war. Politicians talked and called for political solutions.

In the mountains of Sierra Madre on Luzon, Commander Skull was getting ready to up the ante for war over peace.

President Aquino met with the chief of staff of the armed forces. He stood in front of the lady president, dressed in an impressive, well-tailored military uniform. Uniforms and medals did not intimidate this lady.

"General, have the United States offered to assist us?" the president asked.

"We have received no word," answered the general. "But be patient, Mrs. President, it will come when they become aware of our position. When I receive word, it will come from very secret sources. You will be the first and only person to know."

"Word must come soon. Our country cannot be allowed to fall to the godless Communists like in South Vietnam, Afghanistan, and Nicaragua," said the president in an urgent voice.

"No. We will ask for assistance from the United States, but we will not depend upon them for our survival," the general assured her. He wanted to think pro-American, but at times it was very difficult. The Americans had a bad habit of thinking that their money was the answer to all things and the only thing required to keep friends.

"Have you checked with your sources for more assistance from Japan?" she asked, then held up her hand to silence him. "I know the opposition in our country of dealing too closely with the Japanese. Especially when it comes to our national security. But the war has been over long ago, and we have been trading on an economic front for a number of years with the Japanese. There is one thing all should remember, and that is I will negotiate with anyone who will help our country survive."

"The Japanese can help us with finances, but it will take the U.S. to supply us with the proper military equipment and people to train our soldiers," the general insisted.

"Yes. Yes, you are right," admitted the president.

"It would be to our advantage to get money from the Japanese to buy war material from the Americans," the general smiled openly. "We would have less of a threat of being cut off by the U.S. Congress when the going gets rough."

"We need those helicopters," she replied. "They are needed against the NPA."

He agreed with her. The Communists were building forts that were going to be difficult, if not impossible, to destroy by conventional means. A few of the new attack helicopters the Americans had developed would even the odds against a dug-in enemy with air-to-air missiles.

She stood a moment behind her desk, lost in thought with her problems, ignoring the general in front of her.

The general saw that he was dismissed, saluted, and left the room.

The president of the Philippines knew the vulnerability of her position. She was thought of as merely a housewife by many of the Filipino men and even some of her country's women. But the majority of the people had looked to her for leadership after her husband was assassinated. Her power had always come from the people. But the many attempts at coups against her government, her need to call upon the United States for help when threatened, and the lack of reforms the people had called for placed her in a weak position. Self-serving bureaucrats had slowed down or stopped many of the reforms she wished to make. Many of the military leaders were just waiting for her to fall on her face. She had to do something about the growing communist threat, and do it quickly.

The president sat down and wrote an urgent message of a highly classified nature to the president of the United States. She asked him for a number of America's new AH-64 Apache attack helicopters. Her generals insisted they were needed if the government was going to make effective attacks upon the NPA forts. The NPA claimed to have forty-seven heavily armed forts, guarded by antiaircraft missiles and guns they had received from the Moros. The Moros received the weapons from their Islamic brothers, the Iraqis. Her generals informed her that these new helicopters were the only ones with enough armor plating and antimissile electronic equipment to defeat the Soviet-made antiaircraft weapons now owned by the NPA.

The AH-64 was a sensitive, highly sophisticated weapon and the United States hesitated to give it to other countries, even her closest friends. The Philippines had cooled their close relations with the United States since the military installations of Subic Bay and Clark had become a political football. The president of the Philippines was sure that the president of the United States was aware of the significance of the alliance between the Moros and the Communists. This alliance made her government more unstable than it was even under the best of circumstances. With the dreadful economic state of her country, the political opposition, the always-volatile situation in the military, and the unrest of the Moros, her reign was under anything but normal circumstances.

When she had been elected by her people, she had promised to serve only one term. The end of her term as president was near. She wished to see the democratic form of government continue with free elections by the people to determine who would fill the vacant post of president.

The president finished the message. She put down her pen and buried her face in her hands. She was so tired. Oh, Blessed Son of God, it was so much easier being a wife and mother to a husband and children than mother to a country.

General Sullivan followed the aide into the Oval Office. The general stepped into the room and the aide closed the door.

"Sit down, General," the president invited. "Did you have any problems getting the right equipment together?"

"No, sir. All we need is the team leader appointed and the team put together," replied Sullivan. "We have a man in mind."

"I won't ask who. Just get the job done within the guidelines we have decided upon," said the president. "I don't want to have a contra affair with my administration."

"We won't, sir," the general assured him.

"The sooner the team is formed and we get that equipment to the Philippines, the better," the president said. "The general public may not like using covert means to counter an aggressor, but the American people would hate to see the Philippines fall to communism. With the new weapons the Philippine intelligence tells us the NPA now have, they are a threat."

"True, sir. Plus, the NPA owes this country a heavy debt," growled Sullivan. "They've assassinated too many of our people. The brutal assassination of Nick Rowe two

years ago was a kicker. The man I have chosen to head the
team was an old friend and fellow Texan of Rowe. We
won't have trouble finding men to go to the Philippines with
him. Some will say we've waited too damned long."

The president knew Sullivan was complaining about
politicians' inability to protect its citizens or respond to
terrorist acts against Americans in other countries. These
men did not fault their country, but their politicians. Many
were like the general, and felt only a military response was
appropriate.

"Get it done, General. Just keep me informed," ordered
the president. "Congress has given me more powers for
covert work since that Panama fiasco, but they will keep a
close watch. We want to kick ass. But there will be no wild
cowboys. If this gets screwed up and my opposition finds
out, my administration will be crucified."

"That's not going to happen, Mr. President," said Sullivan. He saluted the president and left the room.

Famous last words, the president mused to himself. He
had been in public office for many years. He knew well the
fickle public. They could be for one thing one day and a few
days later be swayed to the other side. But there was one
thing the American public respected and was behind, and
that was use of force to put down some threat they were
completely against. He had heard old military men refer to
it as being a man with a "big set of balls."

A presidential aide met Sullivan in the hall. He told the
general, "You see how important this is, General. The
president of the United States doesn't meet with anyone in
private very often."

"I know. We have about everything ready to assist the
Philippines," Sullivan told him.

"We have to do something in a hurry. The Communist

party is a great threat to the democracy of the Philippines. Plus, our lease time for our bases are about up," the aide stated.

"The administration has Resolution 445 to support the president in giving aid to the Philippines," the general reminded him. "It gives him great leeway to assist in defeating the Communist insurgency, plus get renewed leases for our bases."

"Yes, that's true. But we politicians trust opposition less than the general public trusts any of us," the aide said, smiling.

"We'll do our job," said Sullivan, shaking the man's hand and leaving. He had work to do.

3

Brigadier General Daniel Olive looked up from his desk at the man who walked into his office. A grin of pleasure broke his solemn face as he stood up and walked around his desk. "It's good to see ya, Truck."

"And you, Dan," returned Truck.

The two men met in front of Dan's desk and gave each other a Special Forces bear hug. They stepped back, gripping hard to each other's hand.

Truck Grundy looked at Dan with his one good eye, the color of hard, gray steel. Truck lost his left eye to shrapnel in the Vietnam War, which grounded him from flying army helicopters. He had said at the time that he was lucky he had not lost the right one, which was his "shootin' eye." Truck remained on active duty until 1981 and retired as a lieutenant colonel. He was a tall man, barrel chested, and his gray hair was cut in a military fashion. He had a Texas accent and he was as big and tough as Texas itself.

"Ya got those choppers ready, Dan?" asked Truck.

"Well, damn, Truck, can't we at least have a short visit?" Dan wanted to know, punching a button on the telephone and ordering, "Two mugs of airborne coffee, black."

"I didn't know anything else was served here on Smoke Bomb Hill," commented Truck. He walked to a chair and sat down.

Dan followed and took a chair across from him.

An aide-de-camp brought in two mugs of coffee and placed them on a small table between the two men. He left, not waiting for a command.

"You still got your headquarters in San Antonio?" asked Dan.

"Yep. My sister takes my messages, pays my bills, and controls my bank account," Truck informed him. "That leaves me free to pursue my first and greatest love—war. There's always one going on somewhere."

"That seems to be a fact," admitted Dan. He looked into Truck's good eye. "I thought you and your first wife was gettin' back together."

"She's interested in gettin' back together. I ain't," Truck said bluntly. "She lives in Killeen, right outside Fort Hood. I see her every once in a while. Dot's between husbands now. The old gal's getting too old to be kicking out husbands. She lets me come by to wear off my passion now and then."

Dan shook his head and smiled. He knew Truck's first wife, and one of his friends had been married to her. She was a hard woman to know, and he would hate to try to live with her. He understood why Truck broke up with the woman years before. He had known Truck's second wife, a Korean woman, who had died a few years back. That one was a fine lady. Together they had had one daughter.

"You're ready to go to work, I see," said Dan. "But hell, what's so unusual about that? When you come by here and ya tell me you're satisfied with life, that's when I'll worry about ya."

"I've told my team to meet me at Fort Hood. When I leave Bragg, I'll go straight for there," Truck informed him. "I just hope those Air Cav boys have got that equipment ready."

"They'll have everything ready. I've made contact with the AF Air Commandos and they'll fly you anywhere in the world you want to go," Dan assured him. "When you get to Hood, a colonel will give you an update briefing on the Philippines. At that time, give him a list of anything you might need. He'll keep your needs updated."

"Goddamn, do we have to req toilet paper like we did in Laos?" asked Truck.

"Yep. All requisitions will be classified as 'secret.' This is a very sensitive program," Dan reminded him.

"Okay. Everything's classified 'secret' or higher and will be transmitted by code names only, and only on a need-to-know basis," muttered Truck. "Just like Laos. We'll also be 'sheep-dipped,' I suppose?"

"Yep," said Dan, then grinned and added, "Just like Laos."

"Sheep-dipped" meant all the active-military-duty personnel would be taken off active military rolls and disappear from society. The Central Intelligence Agency would place their names in their files to provide the men with insurance from their insurance company. When the active-duty men returned to duty, whether it be one year or ten years from now, they would return with a rank keeping up with their contemporaries. This system kept them covert and from having any connection with the United States government. If you had to go covert, do it right.

"The president wants this thing to work in the worst way," said Dan. "We've gotta start helping our friends or we might as well say, 'Good-bye, it's been good to know ya.' I don't like that idea."

"If you want to keep it from the U.S. Congress and the news media, there's things you gotta do to keep the world from knowing about it—like keeping it secret. You also gotta keep the enemy from knowing about it. That is until you're ready to kick 'em in the ass," Truck gave the simple answer. "Keep things covert an' give your men a chance to live."

Dan hated to run business that way, but he knew Truck was right.

Truck had been in the business of working for his country for over forty years. He fought his first war as an eighteen-year-old trooper in the infantry in the Korean War. At age fifty-seven, he had been around the block many times. That block included North and South Korea, Indochina, Central and South America, Africa, the Middle East, behind the Iron Curtain, and places most people had never heard of, or would dare go. He had been there as a soldier and also as a retired army officer and agent for his government. But he had always been there for one main reason—he was a warrior and was always hunting a war. If all wars ended, which he knew was impossible, then he wondered what in the hell Truck would do then. A boring thought, so Mack "Truck" Grundy, lieutenant colonel, U.S. Army, retired, never thought about it.

"I'll be your control, Truck. Only those in a 'need to know' will have this info," Dan told him.

"Bad Bear will know the code name," Truck informed him.

"You and Bad Bear still runnin' together, eh?"

"As long as we got any runnin' left," replied Truck. "We've been around the pike together. If it hadn't been for him, I'd be dead a couple of times over."

"That big Indian would do anything for you. You'll do anything for him," said Dan.

"That's what you call blood brothers—without sheddin' the blood." Truck gave a rare grin, then asked, "Who's gonna be my one-on-one?"

"Rufus Holguin. You know him," said Dan.

"Yep, since he was a captain," said Truck, placing the empty mug back down on the table. "He knows I don't like much of this one-on-one business. The less we meet, the better it's gonna be."

"He knows that," Dan said. He knew Truck liked to operate on a long rope. He had done all right so far in this covert business, so he and Sullivan would let him run.

"Dan, here we sit, wasting time when I could be gettin' them boys together and doing business," complained Truck.

Dan grinned at Truck's impatience. Age still had not slowed his old friend down. "You going to stop by the SF Memorial while you're here?"

"Yeah, I've got a few friends listed on the wall. On the black wall in D.C., and the wall out there," said Truck, standing up and holding out a large hand.

"I know you have luck already, but good luck, Truck," said Dan, shaking the older man's hand with warmth. "The old guys, the characters of this army, are dying off. We don't want to lose you at an early age."

"I'll second that," Truck said, and headed for the door.

"Hey, you using a taxi to get around?" asked Dan.

"Yep."

Dan walked to the door. His aide and his three-stripe sergeant staff car driver stood up. "Sergeant, this man has the use of my sedan. Take him where he wants to go, then take him out to the airport for his plane. If you're late, I'll have someone else take me where I want to go."

"Yes, sir." The sergeant put on his headgear and ran for the door.

"Thanks, Dan," said Truck. He raised a hand as he departed.

Dan looked at his aide. "See that man? If he wants something, you get it. I don't care if you have to shoot a general to get it, just do it."

"Yes, sir," the first lieutenant answered. He watched the general walk back into his office and close the door. These old-time troopers stuck together and were not concerned about what others wanted or thought. Maybe he would be part of a closed society like that someday.

Truck walked up to the Special Forces Memorial and stood a moment before entering. He was not the teary, emotional type, but this was different. This place had been set up by the Special Forces Association and other Special Forces people and their supporters to honor their war dead. Business like that was of an emotional nature. This memorial, the "Black Wall" in Washington, D.C., and the blowing of taps would bring tears to Truck. He would stand with his brother warriors, or alone, and let the tears flow down his cheeks. He knew that when the last note of taps was played, other tough old warriors would be wiping their eyes with the backs of their hands and handkerchiefs.

He walked back to the general's sedan and the driver drove him to the Special Operations Command operations section.

The Operations Officer of SOCOM was waiting for him. The colonel handed Truck a packet of maps and papers marked Top Secret. They would fill Truck in on the situation in the Philippines and make him aware of some of the contingency plans SOCOM had for that area.

Truck took the packet and walked to a table. He laid out the information and started to read.

Two hours later, he returned the packet to the colonel, thanked him, and left. He was ready to get to Texas and Fort Hood.

Truck listened to the jet engines whine and felt the airplane shake from the air currents they were flying through. He had spent many hours flying over the world and had developed a traveler's attitude about flying: Lean back, sleep as much as possible, and keep yourself from going nuts while sitting and waiting.

Lieutenant Colonel Michael "Truck" Grundy, U.S. Army, retired, was a lanky, big-boned man with powerful hands and huge shoulders. He had always been interested in keeping himself in good physical condition and ran a couple of miles every morning. He was six feet and one inch of fighting infantryman, paratrooper, and Green Beret, and stood two inches taller with his cowboy boots on.

He had been in the army since the Korean War, where he fought as a rifleman and squad leader in the infantry. He had gotten his commission in the army after the war and received a degree from a university on the "bootstrap" program. His regular-army commission was in the infantry, but he was also a paratrooper, with ninety-three static-line jumps and three hundred free-fall and HALO jumps. Truck always thought of a parachute as just an instrument to get a man on the ground to fight. He had done a little sports parachuting, but he did not have as many jumps as his daughter. Linn was a sports-parachute nut in his estimation. He smiled at the thought of his only real love, his only daughter.

He had been a helicopter pilot before he had his left eye put out, but after retirement, having one eye did not keep him from flying contract or from becoming rated for the army's AH-64 Apache. The instruments were a worry to a soldier made of iron and not computer diagrams, but he had mastered the bird.

Truck had been on a number of tours to Vietnam and Southeast Asia during the Vietnam War. He was forced to retire after thirty years in 1981. The army would have forced him out in his twenty-eighth year, but he was doing some highly classified work that kept him active before mandatory retirement. A man with the rank of lieutenant colonel was forced to retire at twenty-eight years, but if an officer made the rank of full colonel or higher, then he could stay on active duty for thirty or more years. Truck felt the army was hurting itself by not keeping their old, experienced soldiers.

After his retirement, Truck had been contracted by the U.S. government to train men in other countries. His Indian friend, Bad Bear, had retired from the army and joined him. They had been on some rough tours in the past nine years, at times fighting to stay alive.

He was looking forward to this new assignment. It would be good to get back to soldiering and war.

The drone of the engines and noise of the wind on the side of the airplane lulled him to sleep.

4

The men in the room were as diversified in appearance as they were in experience and duty service.

Chief Warrant Officer Cliff "Bad Bear" Sate-Zalebay, U.S. Army, retired, Special Forces and helicopter pilot, Vietnam veteran, was an old sidekick and combat veteran with Truck. No matter who worked with the two men and what their ranks, Truck always looked upon Bad Bear as his second-in-command. Bad Bear was an expert in demolitions, weapons, and communications. The tall, six-foot-four-inch, powerful dark man was a Kiowa Indian and a direct descendant of fierce warriors and had kept up that warrior tradition. Bad Bear liked combat, women, and straight bourbon, although not necessarily in that order. He drank beer or anything else when bourbon was not available. Being married twice, the first time to a Kiowa woman and the second time to a white woman, was enough for him. But bad marriages had not put him against all women, just him being married to one.

Lieutenant Johnny "Crackers" Grahame, U.S. Navy, retired, jet-fighter pilot turned helicopter jockey, at thirty-two years of age was the youngest man in the group. Crackers had not been in combat and always seemed to be trying to prove himself. His older brother, a jet-fighter pilot, was shot down over North Vietnam and was still listed as MIA, missing in action. This rode heavy on the tall, lanky man from Indiana. He was a phenomenal pilot and brilliant tactician who loved to relax with mechanics and any gadgetry having to do with aircraft. He carried his basketball with him wherever he went and would challenge anyone to a game at any time. He was retired from the navy for a minor disability and became a helicopter test pilot for Hughes, Boeing, and Bell. He had flown with Truck over the past six years.

Lieutenant Colonel Matty "Red Dog" Bavaros, U.S. Air Force, helicopter pilot and para-jumper, Vietnam War veteran and Air Force Air Commando, was not "fit" to fly with regular air force people. His attitude matched his flaming red hair and the perpetual dour look on his face. His call sign in Vietnam had been "Red Dog." He ate a nearly raw, inch-thick steak every night when he could find one and washed it down with scotch. Even his hardy friends stayed clear of him until he finished his steak. The tall, lanky frame housed long, stringy muscles that were powerful beyond belief. No one had beaten him at arm wrestling. Red Dog looked mad all the time and he usually was. He hated all forms of communism, weak people, the U.S. Congress, and wimpy U.S. Administrations.

Commander Charles "Chuck" Taylor, U.S. Navy, pilot, Vietnam War veteran and ex-POW, flew rescue missions in Vietnam. He was shot down in his Jolly Green Giant on his second tour as a new full lieutenant of two months. Chuck spent four years as a POW in the infamous Hanoi Hilton.

He was near retirement and a promotion to captain. He had volunteered for his last assignment for his country. A quiet, reserved man, he loved his wife and family, who lived in Chicago.

Major Todd "Jumper" Mason, U.S. Army, Special Forces, helicopter pilot and paratrooper, Vietnam War veteran as an enlisted man on his first tour, was from the mountains of Colorado, was the "outbound" type who liked to climb mountains as well as tall buildings, was an expert in survival tactics, and flew anything with or without wings. He was passed over for lieutenant colonel because of the bad publicity and $1,500 fine he received for climbing and jumping off the Sears Tower building in Chicago with a parachute. His wife left him because he spent most of his off-duty time in search of adventure and volunteering for hardship and dangerous assignments. He would do anything for excitement.

Major Steve "The Gooch" Guccine, U.S. Army, helicopter pilot and Vietnam War veteran. The Gooch got out of the army to return to Brooklyn after the Vietnam War. He was a tough street biker before he went into the army, but things had changed since he was a young man, and dope dealers had taken over the streets. After a few gang brawls and a killing, he returned to the army. He was a natural-born pilot.

These were the men Truck had chosen for his team. He personally knew all of them except Commander Chuck Taylor. He had requested them through General Olive. The men still on active duty had been assigned to the Joint Special Operations Command, with headquarters at Fort Bragg, North Carolina.

When the personnel officer at SOCOM had commented about the middle-aged group of old warriors Truck was putting together, Truck stared at him with his one good eye.

The lieutenant colonel ducked his head and returned to business. God, he thought, the stories about Truck Grundy are probably all true.

Truck walked into the room, followed by two men dressed in civilian clothes. One was U.S. Army Colonel Rufus Holguin. The second man was CIA agent George "Matt" Helms.

None of this bunch came to attention.

"Okay, listen up," Truck ordered in his easy Texas drawl. "This man here is my one-on-one. His code name is 'Dusty Road.' I've known him for a number of years, like since Nam. If he tells you something, it's an order that you will live or die with.

"This other feller is a CIA man and will be known to you only as 'George.' He's a good field operator, and he and I have operated with each other for years. If ya trust me, you'll trust him. He's giving up his sneaky-peak time to do a little admin on our behalf.

"Now, these two are gonna tell us something about the Philippines you need to know, and do some personnel business."

Rufus put his briefcase on the table and took a rolled-up map from under his arm. He placed it on an A-frame. He looked at the men. "If any of you don't know where the Philippines are located, you shouldn't be in here."

This brought a chuckle from the men.

He continued, "Here is a quick intel report on the situation there as we know it. President Aquino has got three forces to contend with. One force, led by her vice president, is political and is the business of their country. The second two forces are shooting-and-killing dangerous. There are the Moros, and then there's the New People's Army, known for years as the Huks.

"The Moros in the south control this part of the country shaded in blue."

Rufus pointed to the map.

"They are demanding complete separation and independence from the Philippines. They are trying to take control of Mindanao, along with its natural resources. The natural resources are extensive. The government is holding the smelting and metals-processing plant in Zamboango at present. Zamboango is here"—Rufus pointed to the map again—"on the western side of the island on this narrow peninsula.

"The government also has control of the copper mines in the southeast of the island around Davao. They control the gold and silver mines in the north around Lligan.

"The Moros have made a deal with the Huks, the New People's Army, so they will take control of Mindanao." He paused, then asked, "Ya got that? The Moros have made a deal with the Huks. The Moros have traded equipment to the Huks for land control."

Rufus stopped talking and pointed to the main island, Luzon. "The areas shaded in light red are where the NPA is most active. The areas in dark red are where the NPA have forts located and control the area. You will note that most of the areas they control are in mountainous, jungle regions— The standard guerrilla country we're all used to."

Rufus looked at the men a moment. "Gentlemen, most of you are white-looking round-eyes who are easy targets for Communist death squads to spot. Bad Bear here is too damned big to be taken for a Filipino, so he's also a good target."

"His size makes a better target," growled Red Dog Bavaros.

The men chuckled at Bad Bear's expense.

"So keep all of this in mind when you go out looking for

women and booze," grinned Rufus. "You gotta admit, though, it'll make your shack jobs interesting."

After the laughter, he continued, "The NPA have been targeting Americans for assassination. The main intel I have for the reason NPA gave away their hold on Mindanao is a bitch for you chopper guys," Rufus continued. "In exchange for control over a little territory, the NPA received antiaircraft guns and ground-to-air missiles from the Moros, and the Moros received the equipment from their Islamic buddies in Iraq."

"I told ya we shoulda turned Israel loose on that bunch," Red Dog growled. "Goddamned wimps in State."

"I suppose all of ya know that when Red Dog retires he's gonna get a job with the State Department," commented the Gooch Guccine innocently.

"Gooch, you can be replaced," returned Red Dog.

There were a few catcalls from the men.

Rufus waited patiently. He grinned and thought, And just think, all these guys are middle-aged.

"Are there any questions?" asked Rufus.

There were none.

Matt Helms walked in front of the men and looked at all of them for a moment. "If none of you have heard the term 'sheep-dipped' before, I'll explain it to you. We used it in Laos: The government would take men on active duty and have them assigned to our rolls for duty only. Your files will be taken out of your branch of service and you will, for all practical purposes, disappear from military society.

"Don't worry, you'll be promoted along with your peers."

"Goddamn! Maybe I'll make LTC," commented Jumper Mason.

Matt continued, "All of you will be given insurance with the Company's insurance company. Your dependents will be taken better care of than they would from your military retirement. When you want to leave this program, let us know and you will be sent back to your regular service for assignment.

"Since we're all in a U.S. of A. government agency, ya know we got forms to fill out."

Impolite boos came from the men.

Matt passed out forms to each man. "You retired people go on the same list and with the same insurance company. We want a beneficiary and an alternate listed.

"We will give you an address for your dependents and all business to use when writing you. All mail, I repeat, all mail will be sent to this address. Your return address will be this same address.

"Are there any questions?"

None of the men looked up, finishing their paperwork. Truck, Bad Bear, and Crackers sat and watched the men. The CIA had all information on them from past operations.

When the papers had been returned to him, Matt told them, "Gentlemen, you are now sheep-dipped an' don't belong to nobody, except this beat-up old Texan here."

Truck shook the two men's hands and they left with a wave and calls of departure.

After the men settled down, Truck stood before them. He picked up a sheaf of papers and passed them out. "Boys, this team of ours is called Eagle Attack Team in public. The classified code name for us is Fire Storm. That classification is top secret and already has a designation of 'executive privilege.' Information will be released only at the pleasure of the president of the United States.

"Our choppers have already been checked out from the Sixth Aviation Battalion and are ready to fly. Each of you will have time to fly one of the Apaches to check it out for yourselves. Each of you will be assigned a chopper, but none of you will have to sign for it. There is no paperwork."

"Goddamn, what kinda outfit is this?" asked Jumper in mock amazement.

"We are the lost souls of the air, never to return again to this life," put in Crackers.

"Crackers, shut your fuckin' mouth," spat Red Dog.

Some men were superstitious, fliers being among the most. Saying aloud anything that could be bad was a no-no.

"When we finish training the men in the Philippine Air Force, some of the choppers will be turned over to them. I don't like the idea of giving anybody an Apache. But I'm only an old trooper, not a president. But this may change," said Truck.

"I can't see giving Apaches to nobody. Those things have got too much classified goodies in 'em," growled Bad Bear.

"An old friend, who has made general, is always ahead of the pack. He thought there may be use for a stationary trainer in this program, so he asked those boys who build these things to make one up. The McDonnell Douglas people have given us a stationary trainer to take with us."

He held up his hand to a couple of protests. "I know, most of ya like hands-on training. But, we can keep those things in a hangar at Clark and never have to expose our aircraft before we go to a covert location."

"We're gonna do everything in that hangar and keep our Apaches hidden?" asked Chuck. "Good idea."

Chuck was wild as the rest when he got into the air and behind the controls of an aircraft. But he was a field-grade officer of the sensible type when it came to business.

"The air force will provide us with guards twenty-four hours a day," Truck told them. "No one, including the guards, will be able to go into the hangar without the proper pass. Only we guys, the men we train, and a few other personnel will have those passes. So if ya see anyone hanging around we don't know, or ya don't think belongs, let me know. Or let the APs know.

"We're gonna need more men to round out this team. We need an air observer and a ground man to train ground troops. There's a group of men I know very well who float between Manila and Bangkok. They're professionals all, who have worked for the U.S. before. Some are retired from some U.S. government military service or agency. Bad Bear may get some of them together to train a group of Filipinos as a strike team for para and chopper work. These Filipino troops will not know about the Apaches until we take them to our hidden camp."

Truck looked each man in the eye with his good eye. "You guys should know how I am about some things by now, either personally or by reputation. So that we don't get our wires crossed about how I stand on things, let me give ya some of the more important things I will not put up with. No screwing around the flagpole with local women. Ya can't train and advise a man while you're gumming around on his woman. Ya get something downtown if ya need it. Manila is a big city. A place where everything goes, and it's not around the flagpole. And if ya ain't scared of VD or AIDS, be my guest and go get all the ass you want. Just don't come in screwed out and expect me to have any sympathy.

"I won't have any duty boozers on my team. If ya can't get enough of that stuff at night and off duty, then get another job. I don't want ya around me.

"All of you should know how I am with Bad Bear. We've been running together a long time. I don't give a damn who ya are, I look to him to take care of things when I ain't around. I hear any complaints about how things are between me and him—you go. And one thing more: when I can't handle some tough ass, Bear is my regulator. That goes for anyone on the team or outside our group."

There was no doubt in any of their minds. They did not want, nor would they have, any physical trouble with Truck Grundy. He was known and documented to have killed people with bare hands and knife.

"My code name for this operation is Pegasus, and Bad Bear's is Bugle Boy. Your code name is stapled to the form you are holding. Learn it now and burn it before we leave this room.

"If there's any questions, we'll get to 'em as we go along. I reckon we oughta go on over to the airfield and look our new babies over," suggested Truck.

The men read their code names, took the paper slips to the metal tray on a table, and burned them. They left the safe room and raided the Fort Hood army airfield.

The men looked the Apaches over. The choppers had been painted black with no markings on them except numbers one through six.

The men took out the choppers with the numbers matching those assigned to them for a test flight and took the aircraft through its paces. The airfield commander was present to observe the transfer of the helicopters. He had not signed for any of the aircraft, but he still felt responsible for the equipment.

Crackers Grahame came in for a low-level flight. The noise was deafening. He pulled and pushed levers to do some exotic maneuvers. Not many people could, or would, put an Apache through the paces that Crackers could. He lifted off with a barrel roll, an impossible maneuver while shooting up into the sky.

"He can't do that!" the airfield commander shouted.

"Looks to me like he done done it," returned Truck.

"That kind of flying is against every regulation I ever read," the colonel told Truck, irritation and anger in his voice.

Truck looked at him steadily and said, "Colonel, you take care of your post and I'll take care of mine."

The army colonel walked off grumbling under his breath. He had no idea who this crew was or who they worked for. It was best to keep a low profile on this. His executive officer knew Truck and said he worked on sensitive, covert projects.

The men returned from their test flight, happy with what was given them.

They gathered around Truck.

"The choppers are rigged so we can blow them either by flipping a switch or by direct fire from one of our ships. They won't blow on contact in a crash," Truck told the men, "but we're not gonna have any choppers left behind on a desert floor or the jungle or anywhere else."

The men agreed with that.

"We're taking an all-terrain vehicle with us that must be used to load, reload, and service the choppers," said Truck. "Let's get our gear together. The C-5s will be here soon, and then we're off to the Philippines."

The men unloaded their personal gear from the bus that brought them to the airfield, and all of them lined up their gear in an orderly fashion. Habits are hard to break, and all of them had the habits of military men.

Crackers Grahame took his basketball hoop and basketball and placed them in the helicopter he was to fly. Where he went, they went.

The Gooch told Crackers, "I need a place to put a bike."

"Yeah, the air force carries bikes with them in those big-troops ships," replied Crackers.

"I don't mean a peddling bike. I mean a street chopper. A bike with a motor on it," The Gooch informed him.

Crackers just looked at him and said as he walked away, "Ya need to get a smaller toy to play with."

Truck was ready to get on with the program. He thought six Apaches were a little too much for an operation, but he had not yet gotten control of things. When he did, then he would have some output that the powers-that-be would have to listen to.

He knew his men were among the best in their business, which was not only that of flying helicopters but also of being experts as soldiers. Soldiering was going to be a lost art if the United States people did not do something about the United States Congress. An army may not be needed right now, but what about the future? If the military died down to nothing, so would all the research and development that went along with war. If the military kept being cut back, who would keep up with new tactics and train the young men needed to fight wars for their country? Truck felt that the country might be left behind in the defense department so that more food stamps could be bought. Those people who thought peace had dawned and the cold war had melted were not going to be well regarded by their descendants when they found that they could not defend themselves. Truck believed world peace was about as feasible as duck shit in a pond was for curing world hunger.

The men were ready when the C-5s landed. So were their birds of war, the U.S. Army AH-64 Apache helicopters.

5

The two C-5s landed at Clark Air Force Base, Philippines, shortly before 0100 hours. The control vehicle led the two huge aircrafts across the dark airfield to a restricted area. For many years, Clark had been the jumping-off point for classified projects going to Asia. The U.S. military facility was prepared to handle anything of a highly classified and covert nature.

The first aircraft pulled its nose up close to the open doors of a huge hangar. Its clam-shell doors opened and the ramp that led into the huge maw of the craft came down.

Air force personnel entered the aircraft with front loaders and other heavy equipment and unloaded the three AH-64 Apaches and one trainer. Hughes had designed the AH-64s so they could be dismantled to fit in a C-5 to be transported to distant lands. It would not take long for the air force maintenance crews to get the helicopters ready for flight. The all-terrain vehicle used to refuel and reload the Apaches was driven out and into the hangar. Armament for the three choppers was unloaded and placed beside the assigned aircraft. Only six highly classified Hellfire antitank missiles were unloaded. These would be controlled by the Americans. They would only be used on Truck's orders in a set situation.

The empty C-5 was pulled away and the second one was moved to the hangar to be unloaded. The remaining three AH-64s and armament were unloaded.

Truck stood with a passive look on his stern face and watched with his good eye.

Bad Bear stood with an intimidating stance, making the young airmen nervous as they passed by the large, dark figure. They were glad he was not their section sergeant.

Each team member followed the bird to which he was assigned and looked after it as if he were attached to it by signature. These men were professionals, and each piece of fighting equipment was to be handled with proper care, kept oiled, cleaned, and sharpened.

Crackers went to a chopper and pulled out his basketball net and ball. He called out, "Hey, somebody got a ladder?"

The air force sergeant shook his head in a negative.

"I wanna put up my hoop. There's plenty of room in this hangar," said Crackers.

"Hold on, sir," a young airman told Crackers. He left and went outside.

After a moment, they heard a truck start up and ease into the hangar. The airman stuck his head out the window of the two-and-a-half-ton truck and asked, "Where ya want your hoop, sir?"

Crackers looked the wall over and pointed to the spot.

The airman eased the nose of the truck up to the wall.

Crackers jumped up on the hood of the truck and reached down for The Gooch Guccine to hand the hoop up to him. He took out a tape measure, measured off the distance from the floor to the proper height, and hung up the hoop. When he finished, he jumped off the truck.

"Thank ya, young soldier, I appreciate it," said a satisfied Crackers.

The airman backed the truck out of the hangar, and the air force sergeant cleared the building of his men.

"Anybody wanna play a game?" called Crackers.

Bad Bear looked at him in disgust. "You gotta be plumb outta your fucking gourd. I'm tired. All of us are tired."

"What! Ya ain't been doing nothing but laying on your ass, sleeping and eating all the way from Texas," Crackers reminded them.

"Shove that thing where it ain't gonna get any light, Crackers," The Gooch told him.

Crackers looked at the ball, then said, "I don't think I brought along enough Vaseline."

When the hangar was cleared of all air force personnel, the doors were closed, locked inside and outside, then bolted with large steel pins. These doors would not be used again until they were to leave for their secret camp.

There were no skylights and no windows in the hangar. The only light in the huge, open building came from electrical lights. This hangar had been used for classified equipment many times in the past.

At one end of the hangar were offices, a large classroom, storage rooms, and a latrine with two shower stalls. Truck would like to have set up quarters in the hangar, but it would be too close to work for the men. The men needed rooms to themselves as long as he could get them.

Dawn was breaking and the sun would soon rise.

"The major said that's our bus over there," Truck told the men. "He'll go with us to see we get our rooms assigned and show us the officers' mess. Our quarters will be within walking distance of the hangar. We'll have three jeeps assigned to us later.

"Let's put our gear in our rooms and get some chow."

This was greeted with approval.

Truck gave the men two days to get ready for the students and get acclimated to the Philippines. Lesson plans were prepared or old ones were modified for their new job. Advice was given when called for. He noticed that the men worked well together and were eager to get on with the job. Their morale was high at the beginning. He was interested in seeing how it would stand up after a few days—or weeks—working with people trying to kill them while learning the trade.

The only possible conflict would come from Bad Bear and The Gooch. For some reason there was an instant conflict between the two men. Truck thought that maybe The Gooch felt intimidated by the huge Kiowa and it bothered his macho psyche. He knew the two men were professionals and he would not have any problem from them. He doubted that Bad Bear was even aware of Gooch's feelings. Bad Bear did not worry much about anything— especially conflict from another man.

It was Friday night. The men took a shower, changed into civilian clothes, and found their way to Mary's Panther Bar. The Panther Bar was a hangout for old Asian hands who just never quite made it back to the States after the war or retirement. Others went home but could not stand the noise of civilian life and the States.

This was the end-of-the-week night and the bar was hopping. Young marines assigned to the U.S. embassy and Subic Bay a few miles away could be picked out by their short haircuts and shined shoes. Navy men with that salty look could be easily picked out. The air force personnel could be picked out because most of them were young.

Panther Hyatt sat in a wheelchair at a table eating a late-evening meal. Nothing but a shell was left of a onetime legend of Asia. He was a tough man who had risen from a young heavy-equipment operator in the old days to a master of the new age of technology in the construction field. He had worked for the U.S. government in the Pacific during World War II, hitting the beaches with or ahead of invading army and marine units. He bragged about one beach landing when he and his crew with three 'dozers and two road graders were drinking a cool one when the marines landed.

He had worked in China, Korea, Japan, Vietnam, and other countries of Indochina. But complications of tuberculosis of the bone and joints regulated him to a wheelchair. He owned this bar, and men passing through from all over the world stopped to say they had been in the Panther Bar. Pictures of old Asian hands filled every inch of wall space. Some of the men were CIA, military intelligence, Green Berets, all military services, but all were friends and admirers of Panther Hyatt.

Panther was in pain most of the twenty-four hours in the day, but he had taken care of himself and others all his life. A little disability was not going to deter him from finishing out his life as he had always done—paying his own way.

The old man not only paid his own way, he took care of extended families of the women he had married over the years, and he was a soft touch for old Asian hands in need.

Truck walked over to the table and stood, waiting for the old man to look up. They had been friends for a number of years.

Panther finished putting the food in his mouth and looked up to see Truck. His expression did not change as he finished chewing his food. His body was bent but his eyes were still clear and sharp. His voice was strong. "Well, I'll be damned. If it ain't Truck Grundy in person."

Truck put out a hand and took Panther's frail one. He did not squeeze it as he once would have. Panther had a strong grip in his younger days that could put men to the floor. Truck told his old friend, "Panther, I see you're still taking care of things."

" 'Til I die, Truck. Till I die," assured Panther. He called to a woman near the bar. "Mary, we've got a visitor, an old friend."

Mary walked over to the table. She looked up at Truck. "Well, well, it's been a long time, Truck. Glad you came by for a visit."

"Whenever I'm close, I'll stop by," he informed her.

Mary was a short, well-built Filipino woman from one of the provinces in northern Luzon. She was in her late thirties or early forties. She had married Panther to take care of him in his remaining days. When he died, she would have a place of her own for the time she spent taking care of him. It was an acceptable way for most Asians. Some Americans may not understand, but Asians did, and their friends approved of the arrangement.

"I'll get one of the girls moving," said Mary, and left.

"Is that your crew back there?" Panther asked.

"Yep," Truck said, smiling. "And don't tell me they're middle-aged. I done figured that out."

"You in business?" asked Panther, not prying, just asking.

"Yep. I need a good medic and ground man," Truck informed him. "And I could use a light aircraft man."

"I know two guys you've worked with before," said Panther. "One or both of 'em should be in here tonight if they're in country. One's old Willie Falloure."

"Good. I heard he was in the Philippines and I wanted to

make contact. I'll join the boys and have a few," said Truck. "It's great to be drinkin' San Miguel again."

Truck walked to the two tables the team had pulled together. Beer was already on the table waiting for him. He picked up his bottle and toasted, "Here's to good friends, and to hell with the rest."

"I'll drink to that," came from around the table.

They sat, played with the bargirls trying to pick up a little trade, and enjoyed the change in atmosphere.

A tall black man walked into the room, called a greeting to Panther, and joined a group of men at the bar. He was a powerful man but beginning to spread at the gut from retirement, too much beer, and middle-age. His hair was shot with gray and cut short, airborne style.

"See that man that just walked in?" Truck asked Crackers as he pointed out the black man.

"Yeah. That big black dude," answered Crackers.

"Go over there and tell him there's a Texas boy over here that's ready to teach him where his black-ass place in life is supposed to be," said Truck.

"Are you kidding me?" asked Crackers. "He just might kick my ass out the door before he comes for you."

"Just go tell him," urged Truck. "You're a tough guy and a professional, ain't ya?"

Crackers took another look at the big man, downed the rest of his beer, and walked over to him.

The men at the table could see Crackers talk to the man, standing back at a safe distance, and point to their table.

The black man slammed his bottle down on the bar and lumbered over toward them. He looked like a huge, black bear on a charge.

Truck stood up and walked around the table toward the black man. He stopped, reached into his pocket, and laid his Fifth Special Forces Group challenge coin on the table.

The big black man stood a moment, his dark eyes boring into Truck's. He reached into his pocket and pulled out his First Special Forces Group challenge coin and slapped it down on the table. The black man said, "Ya ain't gonna get me to buy the beer."

Truck nodded in agreement.

"Well, goddamn!" bellowed the black man and strode to Truck on long legs.

The two men met, hands clasped in a handshake, and embraced each other with a big Special Forces bear hug.

"Can I say your name out loud, Truck?" asked the black man, looking around the bar.

"Only low, Willie," said Truck. He looked around the table.

All the Special Forces personnel pulled out their challenge coins and placed them on the table. They were all accounted for.

"I reckon I'll buy the beer for doubting," said Truck. He told his men, "Make room for this man."

A chair was brought up and Willie was seated.

Truck introduced Willie to the men. "Command Sergeant Major William Willie Falloure, U.S. Army, retired, Special Forces, and a few other things. This guy was sheep-dipped in Laos and worked with the Meo tribesmen. His code name was Black Panther. No, the bar is not named for him. It's for that guy in the wheelchair."

"Yeah, old Panther over there use ta be one bad cat, no doubt about it," put in Willie. He looked around at the men. "I see ya still got a red Indian in the bunch. Ya needs a little black to add color to this bunch."

"*Hatscho.* Glad to see ya, Willie," Bad Bear greeted him.

"You, too, Bad Bear," Willie said with a smile. "I'm glad to see the colonel still got you to look out after him."

"Poor old guy needs somebody. And he's my *pah-bee*, so I reckon I been elected," the huge Indian said with a grin.

The men talked awhile and then broke up to mingle with the crowd. Some left, in twos or more, and went to other places of "business." Truck told them that they had best run in pairs when off the base. Hit teams were looking for "round-eyed" Americans.

Bad Bear sat at the end of the table, arms folded across his chest, watching the men around him. He would say nothing. He would drink, pass out if he got enough to drink, and wake at dawn the next morning clear headed and ready to go.

It always ticked Truck off the way the man could put away his booze, get roaring drunk, then wake the next morning without the normal hangover of other men. Truck died a slow death all day after a big bout with a bottle. That was one reason he had slowed down on drinking in his middle years. Truck hoped no one challenged Bad Bear to a fight. The Kiowa went stark raving wild when he was drinking.

"Can I ask what you're doing here, Colonel?" asked Willie.

"Yep," replied Truck, taking a drink from his bottle. "I've got a project here in the Philippines."

"Might there be a place for me?" Willie questioned.

"I was hoping you'd be interested," Truck answered with a smile.

"God! I can't take much more of this simple, easy life. These civilians and their boring life are driving me up the wall," complained Willie. "I'm more than ready."

"I need a ground man. We'll have about twenty to thirty men to train for a strike force," Truck informed him. He knew the old trooper would jump at the chance and would never ask how much the pay was or what the mission would be; just as long as it was a military adventure and exciting.

"My new wife's Filipino; young, too," Willie said, grinning. "She's afraid of them Huks like everybody else. I won't have no trouble going."

"Don't tell her our mission, Willie," ordered Truck in a firm voice. "It's sensitive and classified."

"Oh, no, Colonel, I won't give her no specifics," Willie assured him. "I'm just married to her 'cause she's young and a damned fine-looking woman. And, man, what tits! But I don't trust her with everything."

The two men grinned. Truck understood.

"I'm sorry 'bout your wife dying, Truck. She was a fine woman," said Willie.

"I miss her," said Truck.

"Where's that little gal of y'all's?" asked Willie.

"Linn's out in California flyin' planes and jumping. Why in the hell anyone'd want to live in California and do anything is beyond me," growled Truck. Linn was the only soft spot in Truck's heart. "She flies stunt in biplanes and is one of the best pilots I've seen for her age."

"I'd like to see that little gal, even if it was in California," laughed Willie. "We ole country boys from Alabama and Texas is 'fraid of places like California."

"Ain't that a goddamned fact." Truck gave another one of his growls.

A commotion came from another part of the bar. The dance girls had stopped performing to watch the struggle going on. Men stood around a table in the corner of the room, urging on a certain arm wrestler they had bet on. The man taking all comers was a big U.S. Navy man in his late twenties. He wore a T-shirt with an aircraft carrier on the front. His muscles bulged and nearly ripped out the arms of his shirt when he strained against an opponent.

The tall, lanky Red Dog Bavaros stood behind the men,

watching, but not joining the throng of men. After a while he walked back to the table and sat down to drink more San Miguel beer. Red Dog was a loner. He sat at the table alone, even with others around him.

A roar went up. The sailor stood up and told the room, "Saturday night is the big night. I'll take on anyone with big enough balls to challenge me. Bring your puny little arms and money for the match."

Men cheered. It was a night worth waiting for.

Red Dog drank from his bottle and eyed the sailor. There was a slight smile on his ruddy face.

"I need an observation-plane driver," Truck told Willie.

"The best is here in Manila," Willie told Truck. "None other than old Bo himself."

"Bo Peep Day?" queried Truck.

"Yep."

"I heard he was deep in the bottle," said Truck, ordering more beer.

"This'll get him out. An', Truck, he's worth it. I ain't never seen a better Bird Dog driver than that man," Willie said, his voice filled with admiration. Willie was another ground-pounder admirer of the pilots who flew the light observation plane called the O-1 or O-2 Bird Dog. The jet-fighter pilots just hauled the ordnance to location. The Bird Dog drivers stayed on station, gave the men on the ground company, took hits from ground fire, and told the jet jockeys where to unload.

"Okay. You know where to find him?" asked Truck. He would trust Willie to know what he was talking about. There were sergeant majors who were like generals—they just had the rank, but not much at everyday soldiering— then there were sergeant majors like Willie, who knew what they were doing and saw that things got done.

"I'll bring him out to Clark Monday morning, sober and

ready to go," assured Willie. "He knows how ya are about drinking on duty. He'll stay sober, 'cause now he'll have a reason to."

Members of the team started drifting back to Panther's.

Near midnight, most of them followed Truck by getting a cab and returning to Clark. They had work to do the next day and a big night ahead of them. They had big money to place their bets on a member of their team in the arm-wrestling match. It was going to be a good night in Manila.

6

Commander Skull, the nom de guerre for Casto Burgos, was a large, powerful man with black hair and a dark complexion. Like many Filipino families over the centuries, he was not from one tribal group. He was a mixture of Ilongot, Chinese, and Spanish.

He was a mean, short-tempered man with a streak of cruelness that even his closest followers feared. Yet he was gentle and giving to children and the poor. Very few men are all bad.

Juan José, a member of the Central Committee of the Communist Party of the Philippines–Marxist-Leninist, known to the world as Huks—had been delegated by the committee to meet with Skull and try to convince him that he was wrong in forming military units to contest the strength of the Filipino military. He was to be told that he would bring on the wrath of the entire military and the common people of their country if he kept killing his fellow citizens.

Juan did not like the idea of having a face-to-face talk with this rebel leader. He did not like to have to come into this jungle mountain stronghold to see him. He would rather stay at home in Bayombong and just complain about the man. Also, he was getting too old to climb mountain trails and live the life of a guerrilla. Skull had sent two young men to lead him up the mountainside to the fort on foot, and not by road and an automobile. Skull had said it was too dangerous. Juan was still angry about that.

Juan cleared his throat and told Skull, "During World War Two, when the Japanese invaded our homeland and butchered our people, we Filipinos formed a group from our Communist organization to fight the Japanese. We were the People's Anti-Japanese Army, which was called in the Tagalog language Hukbong Bayan Laban'sa Hapon, and became known as the Huks. In 1946, long before you were born, our name changed to the New People's Army, called Hukbong Mapagpalaya'ng Bayan. We thought we would win a victory over the traditional government, the pawns of the Americans. Our people were killed and driven to the mountains and bush by the Americans and Filipinos. Many turned to banditry and stole and murdered many of our own people. It has taken years for us to get rid of that image of being nothing but thieving, murdering bandits."

Skull broke in and growled, "I am a student of the University of Manila. You don't need to give me lessons in my country's history or that of the People's Party."

"I know, I know. But I am reminding you of how it was with us," Juan told him. He had a story to tell and he was going to tell it. "The Communist Party of the Philippines we have today was formed in 1968 by our great leader José Maria Sison. He believed in the Chinese way of communism. He sought to bring us together as a party of the people, not as bandits. It has been a long, hard struggle to get people to think of us as a party."

"I know who Sison is, old man. He taught at the university where I went to school," interrupted Skull again.

Juan continued, ignoring Skull's continuous interruptions, "We are now becoming more accepted by the common people, the ones we must have behind us. If we start the fight against the Quezon City government too strongly, then we will lose the common people once again. The people will be forced to fight against the government. We all know that it is the common people, the young and old, who die in armed conflicts. It will make many of them turn against us. All we of the Central Committee are saying is for you to go slow. Be sure you have a chance of winning before you get in too deep."

"Our leader, the great Sison, is now in exile and lives in comfort while we live in the mountains and jungles. He tries to gain an alliance with the Soviets. I am a follower of Mao. I don't wish to have anything to do with the Soviets and I will not. But he seems to be willing to deal with anyone just for money.

"And I know, the times have passed for you old men to live in the mountains and fight for the people's revolution. Now you wish to sit at home and play with your grandchildren. That is good for you," agreed Skull. "But do not speak of staying at home with folded hands to us young ones. We still have fire in our guts and desire to rule the land. We will have our chance. If we blow it, like you did, old man, then so be it. But at least we will have had our day."

Juan stood a moment. How could he counter that? The younger man had a point. It was a great point for those who still believed in the cause. "Skull, there is another point I must bring up. We are worried about your dealing with the drug cartel. That stuff, *shabu*, is a very wicked drug. It will destroy many minds and bodies. And the drug cartels will become stronger and we will not be able to root them out."

Shabu was crystal methamphetamine and said to be more addictive than crack made from cocaine. It was a powerful, mind-altering drug. The Philippines was becoming a power in the drug industry and taking the place of Colombia and Hong Kong. This fact scared many of the country's leaders, both of the Communist opposition as well as the government in power.

Skull laughed. "When I have used them for what I want and finished with these people, then I will do like our teacher, Mao and China, and execute all drug users and dealers."

"Then I cannot change your mind about the madness you are leading your men into?" asked Juan.

A dark frown wrinkled Skull's forehead and he glared at Juan. "Old man, I have let you come here because of your age as an elder and because you have fought the fight for so many years. But do not think I will let you belittle me and my ideas without bringing justice upon you for your words."

"Oh, no, I do not make little of you," Juan said quickly. "We of the committee only wish for you to be aware of where you may be taking the rest of us."

"Bah!" scoffed Skull. He looked at Juan. "I have work to do, old man. I'll have a jeep take you back home."

"I would appreciate the ride," Juan said with an appreciative feeling. He would not be able to walk back down the mountain. It had drained all his strength to make the climb in the first place.

Without another word, Skull turned his back on Juan.

Juan walked out of the command post, which was in a bunker, and followed the driver of the jeep. They got into the jeep and left for the ten-hour ride to his home. It had taken him two days to walk up the mountain. God! How had he made such a trip? He knew it would be his last.

Two hundred men were assigned to Skull's mountain fortress at all times. Another five hundred were camped in the jungles within striking distance. In the lower elevations of the mountains, the forest was so thick with triple tree canopies that sunlight could not be seen from the continuous moist, decaying ground. The camps dotting the mountain were hidden from the air by their natural camouflaged canopy. The men lit fires for cooking and heating water only at night. The fires could not be detected from the air at night. Skull ordered no fires during the day because smoke could drift up through the trees and give them away. These men were accomplished guerrillas.

Skull's main fort was near the top of the mountain. It sat in a clearing that woodcutters had used at one time. The small huts on the edge of the clearing had been used for many years by woodcutters and hunters. Now it housed Skull, some of his leaders, and the newly acquired antiaircraft guns.

Bunkers were hidden under the cover of the trees. There were a few open trenches connecting the bunkers, but most of them were connected by tunnels. Tunnels also connected the huts with the bunkers.

Skull called the group into his main briefing bunker. He had called a meeting with these people before Juan arrived. It had been delayed and now the meeting was running late.

He looked at his people, made up of both men and women. These were his propagandists. Some were young, in their early twenties, but his best workers were in their mid- to late thirties. They were the believers, the organizers. The people in this group would leave the mountains and return to their home provinces and spread the word, and that word would be any he gave them. The young believers made the best fighters. They would more quickly give their lives for a cause.

"Power to the people," announced Skull.

The same cry was answered by the assembled members of his group.

"I want a great propaganda move to stop the Aquino government from renewing agreements with the Americans to keep those two military bases on Filipino soil," Skull told the men and women he was meeting with. "Clark and Subic Bay are an affront to the people of the Philippines. They also have three more bases that go unspoken of. They also have the John Hay Air Station in Benguet Province, and Wallace Air Station in La Union Province. Worst of all, they have the Naval Communications Station in Zambales Province. That place is a place of nothing but spies. CIA spies use it to communicate all of their illegal activities all over Asia. They are a shame to our people. We must rid our country of that shame."

The men and women nodded their heads in agreement.

"As long as there is an American presence in the Philippines, the central government can use all of their power to try to eliminate us. We must get rid of the American bases so we can continue our fight against the Aquino government. We must be free to go where we want in our own country to preach the cause of our party," Skull informed them.

"If we attack those bases and show the people that the great paper tiger can have his tail pulled, the people will follow. The people are ready to get the imperialist Americans out of our country. The people are even more angry at the imperialist act of the Americans when they ordered their jet fighters to join the government forces against the coup attempt on the Aquino government. That was an act against our nation's sovereignty," Skull informed them. "Many people have told me that they wish for the Americans to leave our country. They can take their military and capitalist civilian companies home with them. 'Leave us alone! Get out of the Philippines!' is the call we Filipinos have for them."

"Agreed," one man shouted.

"We will guide our people to our own destiny. We will no longer look to or listen to the decadent Americans," said Skull. "We are our own saviors. And we must show the people how to drive the imperialist invaders off the soil of our motherland."

He watched them as they nodded their heads in agreement. They were ready. They would give all they had. Skull had learned well how to fire people up in the schools he had attended in China. He knew the key words to use to bring out the emotional patriotism deep in their souls.

"Go. Go spread the word. Tell our people that they must help the Aquino government change their minds about renewing the treaty that will leave the American military in the Philippines. You will do that by spreading the word that we must rid our country of the American bases. We must force them out and force the government not to renew their leases." He turned from them to hurry their departure.

After they left, he looked at Mano Garcia, his second-in-command.

"Shall I get the attack moving?" asked Mano.

"Yes. By the time you get all the people together, it will be time. Our propagandists have been doing a good job. We are ready," said Skull, smiling. "And when the air force attacks this mountain, they will have many surprises waiting for them."

Skull paused and a frown creased his forehead.

"Why don't we have some pretty young girls up here?" asked Skull.

"We have some beautiful girls here," Mano informed him. This man is unpredictable as hell, his mind growled.

"Yes, but I know all of them," complained Skull. "Send out the word that we need some more young women. If the mothers and fathers do not wish to let their young daughters go for the cause, take them."

Mano looked at Skull for a moment. He wondered what complaint Skull could have. He liked little boys as well as women, but maybe Skull was also tired of the same boys.

The men went about their duties, sure that they were on the right road to becoming the new leaders of the country.

Colonel Louders Yniguez, Philippine Air Force and the team's contact, met with Truck at the office in the hangar. He told Truck, "We will have the men here early on Monday morning. There will be six pilots and copilots/gunners. I am sure that you will not bust out more than one or two of these men, if any at all."

"I'm sure they'll all work out," said Truck. "Has a ground crew been chosen for the support vehicle?"

"Yes. We have chosen four of our best sergeants. They are well trained in ordnance," Yniguez assured him.

"Good," replied Truck. Then he asked, "Will I be able to get that O-1E Bird Dog?"

"You will have one, Colonel. It is also equipped with anti-radar equipment," Yniguez told him. "I will have a man fly it here for your use."

Truck did not tell him that he was getting thirty men from the Philippine Army Special Task Force for Counterinsurgency to train for his use. These men came from the First

Scout Ranger Regiment. Keep things as close to the vest as possible, was Truck's motto.

He knew that some of the rangers may have been in coup attempts against the Aquino government, but they were Filipinos first, last, and always. They would fight well against the NPA.

Yniguez left the office and walked out into the hangar, and Truck followed him out.

The Filipino Air Force colonel stopped and looked at the six Apaches with appreciation. His eyes hungered for one of his own. He looked at Truck and said, "One of the bad things about getting older in service, Colonel, is that the younger men get equipment such at this."

"Yep, the younger ones beat us out," Truck agreed with a grin. "But remember, Colonel, we used to do the same thing to the older men in our youth."

"That is not a great consolation," Yniguez said with a laugh. "But it is one I will have to live with."

Truck walked to the front door with him and let him out and locked the door as he closed it.

Well, things will start Monday, thought Truck. Let's party this weekend, because who knows when the next time we'll be free.

7

Panther's was full. Men gathered around the big sailor called Spike. Some of his shipmates stood, money in hand to cover any bet against the fleet's arm-wrestling champion.

Spike had already vanquished one marine challenger and was finishing a bottle of San Miguel when the men from Eagle Attack Team walked in.

Crackers Grahame, money holder for the team, walked across the room and announced, "All right, men, I'm holding five thousand dollars American that says we've got the champion arm wrestler in this bar."

"I'll take two hundred of that bet," a young American called out without hesitation.

Others surged forward to cover pieces of the five thousand dollars.

Crackers was busy writing down names while Jumper Mason collected the money.

"Who ya got there, buddy?" a man called.

"Well, we got us a real winner. Red Dog's his name and

55

whipping sailors' ass is his game," said the retired navy officer. Crackers walked over to Red Dog and raised his hand above his head.

Red Dog Bavaros looked at him with a scowl, jerked his hand loose, and took another drink of beer.

A few amazed laughs came from the men.

"Ya mean your champ is that skinny, red-faced old fart?" a man called.

"That's him," answered Crackers.

"Well, goddamn, buddy, I hope ya brought a sack full of money," a man scoffed.

"I think we can cover 'bout anything you boys can rake up," Crackers assured them. He walked over to the table and smiled. "I think we got some live ones, boys."

"We can cover the bets," Truck told him.

The others agreed.

"Get your bets in," Crackers called. "We'll let Panther hold the money."

That was agreeable with all.

The center of the barroom was cleared and a table was set up with two chairs on opposite sides.

Spike walked to one of the chairs with a swagger and an air of confidence. He had never been beaten in all of his twenty-eight years of living. This old middle-aged guy was not going to be the first.

Red Dog turned up his bottle, downed the rest of his beer, and sauntered over to his chair, unconcerned and nearly bored with the entire thing. He sat down and looked Spike in the eye and said, "I don't like you, little boy."

A surprised look came over Spike's face, and then he gave a fierce look and growled, "Old man, after I break your fuckin' arm, I'm gonna kick your ass out in the street."

For the first time in days, team members saw Red Dog

give a large, happy grin. "Let's fight, little boy. Ya ain't gonna be able to later."

Red Dog stuck his hand and arm in front of him, crooking his arm and placing his elbow on the table. He held his palm out flat, waiting for Spike to grasp it. His hand was wide and fingers long, but they were not beefy like Spike's ham-size hands.

Spike placed his elbow on the table and paused for a moment, looking Red Dog in the eyes. This old boy was not going to be intimidated. He grabbed Red Dog's hand in a powerful grip and tried to look tough.

The judge came up to the table and said, "Okay. On the count of four: one, two, three, four."

Spike tried to put Red Dog down in one smooth motion.

Red Dog held, his arm as rigid and ungiving as a steel railroad rail that was driven into the ground.

It was at that moment that Spike felt he might be in trouble.

Spike applied pressure.

Red Dog applied just enough pressure to keep their arms straight in the air. His grin grew until all his teeth were visible. It was an unnerving grin.

Blood vessels on Spike's arm grew as his heart pumped blood into the muscles of the straining limb. His jugular veins bulged and his pulse beat strongly. His expression did not change, but he hated the grin on Red Dog's face. After the match he would wipe that grin off the old man's face.

After forty-five minutes of struggle, Spike's friends and shipmates started getting worried. They urged him on, knowing that they would be without women and booze until the next payday if Spike lost. A sailor and soldier lived from payday to payday, as was traditional among armies. But to lose all only two days after payday was more than a young serviceman could take.

"Get him, Spike. He's an old sucker," urged a young sailor.

"I'd rather see a sailor win than that old fart," put in a young marine.

"Damn! I just don't want to lose my money," complained another one.

"Ya ain't gonna lose any. Spike's the fleet champion," another bragged.

Truck sat drinking his beer, unconcerned about the struggle going on at the table.

Willie joined him at his table. "I found old Bo. He was deep in a bottle."

"Where's he now?" asked Truck.

"I've got two sixteen-year-old girls drying him out," Willie grinned. "They're all three in a hot tub, naked as can be. Ole Bo ain't gonna be able to do a thing, but it might make him wanna sober up so he can perform."

Truck laughed with him.

"We gonna win some money?" asked Willie.

"Yep. I ain't seen nobody beat Red Dog. Those skinny, long muscles seem to be made of spring steel," said Truck. Then he chuckled, "That young sailor is in for a surprise."

"I think he's done got surprised," laughed Willie.

Men milled about the room, talking and drinking beer and mixed drinks. Young girls came in off the street and joined the laughing men. It was easier to make a score when men were laughing and having fun. They had yet to learn that if these men lost they would all be broke. Those matters would be addressed when the time came.

Mary and Panther were making money this night.

A girl walked up to Bad Bear. The top of her head barely reached his chest. "You and me go play, okay?"

Bad Bear looked down at her, then, smiling, said, "I don't think you're quite big enough."

"Ah! You come with me I show you I big enough to take on elephant," she shot back at him.

Bad Bear smiled at her. He picked her up with one hand and set her on the bar next to him.

The girl felt the muscle in his arm and then ran a soft hand over his chest. "I think you may be big enough for me to feel it."

Bad Bear gave out a roar so loud everyone turned to look at him. He grinned. "After the bout, we go find out if you talk big or you are big."

She pulled his head to her and stuck her tongue in his ear. She was not interested in the struggling men.

Spike was growing tired. Sweat ran down his forehead and into his eyes. His face was as red as Red Dog's, but the red came from exertion, not natural coloring. This match was going to have to end. He was growing tired and his strength was being drained. The maddening thing was that Red Dog was not suffering from the hour-long struggle.

The young sailor's eyes did not give him away, nor did his muscles quiver and jerk as they got ready to spring. Spike pushed against the older man's arm with all his might.

Red Dog wanted to end this now. He was wasting good drinking time. When Spike gave his final power play, Red Dog applied pressure evenly. His arms seemed to uncoil like a python, his muscles rippling and crawling in their strength. He gave one final grin before he applied a quick jerking motion. The power of the force snapped the wrist of the sailor's arm.

Spike's gasp was heard above the moans and groans of the men around the table. He looked at the bone sticking out the side of his arm, grew white in the face, and passed out, his head dropping on the table and breaking his nose.

Crackers handed Red Dog a bottle of beer. Looking at Spike, he said, "Squeamish bastard, ain't he?"

The redheaded air force pilot downed the bottle in one long pull.

Crackers handed him another bottle.

"If any of you boys wanna play with an old feller again, make sure he's past his prime and can't get a hard-on no more," Red Dog told the young men. He left the table of confrontation and walked over to where Truck and Willie sat. He stood behind a chair to stretch himself and catch up on his drinking.

"We got eleven thousand, eight hundred seventy-five dollars in this sack," called out Crackers.

The losers growled and some cursed their luck.

"It ain't luck, boys. You're little boy done fucked up and challenged a warrior," The Gooch Guccine told the men.

There were a few more growls, but none dared venture calling any of the "old" men out.

Bad Bear walked over to the table, carrying the young woman in an arm as though she were a child. He told Truck, "Boss, I'll be at work on Monday morning."

"Do ya think you'll last that long?" asked Truck.

"I'll give it my best shot," the big man answered, grinning. He walked out of the bar and did not put the girl down until they were out on the sidewalk.

"I'm glad to see he got occupied," said Jumper Mason. "If some of these young 'uns gave him trouble after he got about half-drunk, we'd all had to jump on him to hold him down."

"Drunk Indians do cause trouble," smiled Truck. He had either watched Bad Bear clean out bars or joined him when he needed help. The big Kiowa did not need help very often.

Crackers was a busy man, counting out the money and giving the proper share to the right man. When he finished, he threw a one-hundred-dollar bill in the center of the table. The other men did the same. Truck threw down two one-hundred-dollar bills, adding Bad Bear's payment.

Crackers took up the money and walked to Panther. He put the money on the table in front of the old man.

Panther looked up with a grin. He called to Mary. "Take this money. And this bunch don't pay for drinks the rest of the night."

She smiled happily and walked behind the bar to put the money away and give orders to the bartender and girls.

When the girls saw that none of the young Americans had any money left, they walked over and joined the older men.

"Hey, what's this shit! Can't we get any on credit?" a young sailor called.

"No can do, GI. No money, no pussy," one of the girls called to the men. Then she came out with the universal, "Sorry 'bout that."

"Damn! Ain't this a case. Them old guys got it all. They got all the money, all the booze, and all the women," complained another young American.

"It's back to the base for us, guys."

"Goddamn! Ain't this a case!"

The young men started to drift out of the bar.

Truck looked at the women standing around the table. "Ya know, girls, we just might take ya all on. It might be awhile before we get out again."

One of the girls jumped up and down, her young, unbound breasts bouncing up and down.

"I think I can take a bunch of that," said Jumper.

The men got up to leave, picking out a girl for themselves. The more adventurous picked out two.

"If you don't mind, Truck, I think I'll go back to the base after I finish my beer," said Chuck.

"Yep, I understand, old buddy," said Truck.

"I'll see y'all when you get in," Chuck called after them.

The noise of their passing followed them down the street.

Jumper called down a taxi. One pulled over and he, Crackers, The Gooch, and five girls jumped into the cab. Jumper and one girl got in the front seat. The other six crowded into the backseat.

Crackers came out with a muffled, "You gals give directions."

The girl in the front seat gave an address.

The cab driver put the car in gear and started off. He drove two blocks from Panther Bar when a gunman stepped out into the street and fired into the driver's side of the cab.

The driver slumped over the wheel without a sound. The cab ran into a parked car on the right side of the street.

Two more bursts from an automatic weapon were heard. The girls screamed in fear and pain.

The cab was wedged into a car parked on the street and the doors on the passenger side could not be opened. The Gooch kicked out the window and slipped to the ground. He was followed by Jumper and Crackers. They stood, unarmed but ready to fight if necessary.

But they didn't have to fight. The gunman had disappeared.

"That dirty bastard!" spat Jumper.

The girls were still screaming.

Jumper walked around to the driver's side of the car and opened the back door. The two girls that were jammed up against the seat fell out of the cab and onto the pavement.

Both were dead. They had received the bullets that had been designated for the Americans.

The cab driver was barely alive.

The girl in the front seat was speechless, her vocal cords frozen shut with fright, her eyes glazed over in horror.

"Anyone get hit?" asked Jumper.

"Yeah. You did," said Crackers.

"Huh?" Jumper looked down and checked himself out. There was a small stain of blood across his chest. The bullet had slid across his ribs, breaking the skin but not any bones. "Well, I'll be damned!"

Policemen and ambulances started to arrive.

Crackers, Jumper, and The Gooch spent the remainder of the night either at the hospital or the police station filling out forms.

When it was over and they started back to Clark, The Gooch growled, "I hate them Commies. I'm gonna take pleasure in killing a bunch of them fuckers."

"I can't wait to get my sights on 'em," agreed Jumper.

Crackers just looked disgusted and mean. Finally he grinned and said, "Welcome to the lovely islands of the Philippines."

The other two could not help but laugh with him.

8

The colorfully painted jeep pulled up to the Clark main gate in the early-morning rush and let U.S. Air Force men out. Among the early arrivals was Cliff "Bad Bear" Sate-Zalebay. Although he had spent a weekend drinking hard, he looked fresh and ready to charge for the rest of the week. Except for a change of clothes, of course. From the looks of his bruised and cut knuckles on his huge fists and the lump under his left eye, it was evident that he had also been in a brawl.

He caught the duty bus to a spot within walking distance of his quarters and went to shower and change into duty clothes, which consisted of fatigues with no markings. There was nothing he could do about the lump under his eye, but he did shave the two or three whiskers off his smooth, hairless American Indian face.

One quick check and he headed for the hangar. He was not late, just behind the other guys.

Catcalls and whistles greeted him as he walked into the building.

Members of the team gathered around the big Kiowa.

"Well, was that little thing big enough?" Crackers wanted to know.

"She made me feel like a little boy," answered Bad Bear, breaking out in a grin.

"Was she the one to put that mouse under your eye?" asked Jumper.

"Naw. That was her husband and his brother," said Bad Bear with a shrug of his heavy shoulders. "I don't know what them guys were so ticked off at me about. It's not like I did it on purpose. Hell! I didn't know she had an old man. She even has a kid!"

"I'd like to a seen her when she was pregnant," Jumper put in. "No bigger than she is, she'd be all belly with legs."

"Ya leave the husband and brother alive?" asked The Gooch.

"The brother's okay," replied Bad Bear. "I don't know about the husband. He was trying to hold his guts in with both hands last I saw of him."

"Goddamn! Did ya knife him?" asked a concerned Crackers.

"I took his damned knife away from him," Bad Bear informed him. "A man shouldn't pull a knife if he can't keep it."

The men shook their heads, hoping this would not get him, and/or them, involved with Filipino law.

"Okay, our schoolboys are outside. Let's go greet 'em and show 'em their new toys," called Truck. He was glad all the men in the Philippine military used English as their basic language.

• • •

The Philippine Air Force men were boys to these old troopers who had fought in many countries. But these young men were among the best fliers of their air force. They were members of the 109th Helicopter Company, an elite unit that worked with the army's rangers and the marine's Special Operations teams in counterinsurgency. They were all volunteers, experts in their field and students of a high caliber.

Colonel Yniguez greeted Truck and his men. "We have our best young helicopter pilots here. I am sure that they will learn quickly."

"We'll do our best, Colonel. I'm sure they'll do theirs," replied Truck.

"Each of these men was trained in aviation computers by the McDonnell Douglas Company. Many of the computers they were trained in are carried by the helicopter they will fly," the colonel informed Truck.

"We have a computer expert with us. We'll get it done," Truck told him, and then asked, "Do you wish to stay awhile?"

"No. I'll come back when they get into trainer training," Yniguez answered. "I want to learn how to fly that bird."

With that, Yniguez got into his staff car and left.

Truck walked to the front of the formation. He looked them over, then said, "Men, you will call me Truck. You will learn the names of these other men as we go along. All of them know their job. They are experts. You know nothing. Your ability to fly the UH-1 means nothing. We will teach you all you will know about flying helicopters. Is that understood?"

"Yes, Leader Truck," they answered in unison.

"This area and this hangar is off limits to all except those who wear an identification badge like you have on your left shirt pockets. Even the American guards have the same ID badge," continued Truck. "No one is to know about this place. You are to talk to no one outside your group. You will live, work, and eat within the boundaries you have been assigned. If I see any man I think may compromise what we are doing, I will call Colonel Yniguez and that individual will be placed under house arrest until we are finished with our training. Is that understood?"

"Yes, Leader Truck," they again answered in unison.

"Good. Now, let's get inside and start to work," ordered Truck.

Truck signaled to one of the pilots who was standing ahead and to one side of the formation. "You're the leader of this bunch, Captain Castello?"

"Yes, sir, Leader Truck," the young man answered, and saluted.

"Good. Get the men inside and we'll show them the equipment and the classroom," said Truck.

On order, the men went inside the hangar.

Chuck Taylor introduced the Filipino pilots to the new aircraft they had only heard about but never hoped to be able to fly. They asked the old navy commander many questions about the machine, most of which he told them would be explained in detail as they were trained.

After a look at the helicopters, ordnance, and support vehicles, the men were directed to the classroom, where forms to be filled out were waiting.

Truck walked over to where Willie Falloure stood with Bo Peep Day.

Bo looked wrung out and gaunt from a long drunk. He had malnutrition from lack of a proper diet. Beads of sweat stood out on his pale, waxy-looking skin. His skin reminded Truck of a man taking his last breath before dying. Bo had lost weight during his drunk, but that would come back. His bloodshot eyes were tired, but retained a look of intelligence.

"You gonna make it, Bo?" asked Truck.

"As long as I can make it to the bathroom once in a while," Bo informed him. "I might have to puke a couple a times today."

"Be my guest," invited Truck. "Just as long as you hit the commode every time."

"I ain't gonna mess up the floor, Truck. And I ain't gonna need another drunk. Not while I'm with you guys," Bo assured him.

Truck did not bother to tell him that was a fact, or he would be out on his ass.

After the men were finished with the administration part, Truck gave the first class.

Truck looked the men over as they sat in the classroom. Truck knew that the men were going to have to hump it to handle the computers in this war bird. But he had noticed that many times it was easier to train intelligent men who did not know too much about a subject or piece of equipment than men who had been raised with the technology. Every American kid knew about computers and most had one in his home. By the time the young American was ready to be trained, he already *knew* more about computers than he could be taught.

He had already looked over the records of these men and learned that they were indeed outstanding men in their field. They had sent the cream of the crop.

Among the men were four sergeants, who were designated as the armor crew. The men in the armor crew were outstanding men, led by an old noncommissioned officer who was an expert in ordnance of many kinds. It would not take him long to take command of the support vehicle. He was Penagolawong Sarhento Nino Garcia. *Penagolawong sarhento* was equivalent to the American six-stripe master sergeant E-8.

Truck trusted the old sergeant to do his job, but he wanted an American to take charge of that vehicle. He took note of that problem that was going to have to be addressed.

"Gentlemen, in your folders is information on the Attack Helicopter-64 Apache," Truck informed them, giving them time to look through their folders and come up with the package. He continued, "The McDonnell Douglas–built AH-64 Apache is the most rugged chopper ever built. It was initially made as a tank killer. Its main armament is the tank-killing Hellfire missile. And, gentlemen, it only takes one Hellfire to kill any tank in existence. It is controlled by a laser beam and as long as that laser beam is on a target, you are gonna get a kill. All of that is classified. I will get into its ordnance capability later.

"The Hughes Aircraft Company outdid itself in designing this chopper. McDonnell Douglas did in construction of this aircraft. It costs a lot of money—over eight million dollars a copy, but it's worth it. This bird has two engines. Both are General Electric T700-GE 701s, each worth 1,690 shp turboshafts of power. They will lift the Apache's maximum takeoff weight of 17,650 pounds in a vertical climb of over five hundred feet per minute when it is sitting at four thousand feet altitude on a hot day. Under normal conditions, when loaded with eight Hellfire missiles in its four pods and one thousand rounds of 30mm ammo for its chain gun, it will lift off at about the same speed. With that much ordnance, gentlemen, that's power."

Truck paused to let the men whistle and mull that over.

He continued, "The chopper itself is not only armor plated in the bottom and around its nose and sides, but has a main rotor blade that can stand a hit from up to a 23mm weapon and survive. Those engines and that blade can push the Apache backward or sideways at around fifty-five knots per. It has a max forward speed of about one hundred ninety-six knots. If your transmission runs out of oil, ya still have over thirty minutes of flight time left before it locks up."

Truck paused again to let them soak that information up. He grinned inside. It amazed him every time he talked about the thing. "The Apache is also capable of carrying and firing 70mm rockets. These rockets have different warheads for different jobs. They can be equipped with delayed fuses, which is death on most bunkers. There are armor-piercing rounds, which dismantles light tanks and armored personnel carriers. There are also smoke rounds, which confuse and blind the enemy.

"The company installed what they call a 'Black Hole' system. That thing is an infrared suppressor on the engine exhaust so heat-seeking missiles can't lock in and kill it. That will neutralize most Soviet missiles that we know of."

Truck looked around the room. He had the attention of every man in the room. Their eyes were fixed on him, and if a naked lady passed in front of the room, they just might ask her to leave so they could get on with business. He thought a moment. Well, maybe they were not that interested.

He told them, "To fire all of this ordnance this bird carries, each pilot—the senior pilot sitting above in the rear, and the copilot/gunner sitting lower in the front—will each wear a very special helmet. On this helmet is an instrument called a TADS/PNVS. This stands for target acquisition and designation sight/pilot's night-vision sensor, which enables the pilot to see at night. This TADS/PNVS is coupled to a sight in the nose of the chopper. The sight moves where the pilot looks and the electronic sight optics aim in the direction the pilot moves his head: up, down, or sideways.

The sight has two hundred and forty degrees of movement. It makes the Apache death at night.

"The chopper also has a computer system, which you will get into during classified training, that keeps two choppers from shooting at the same target. One chopper can also identify a friendly even in the dark of night or in a cloud bank."

Truck paused, then continued, "The Apache is easy to reload with ordnance and refuel. That is what that rough-terrain vehicle is for, which you see sitting next to the choppers. A team will be trained to use that equipment. Trained men can rearm and refuel a chopper in a matter of minutes. Without that team, you ain't gonna kill nobody after you shoot your first load. The battle will already be over.

"I have talked enough. We'll take a ten-minute break and then Leader Chuck will give you more on the chopper, Leader Crackers will teach you about the computers, and Leader Red Dog will teach you on tactics. Your days will be full. Learn all you can. I do not know how many of these AH-64s will be left with the Filipino government, if any. That is up to politicians, not we soldiers.

"Take ten."

The men got up and some wandered away from their desks to talk to others. Most sat at their desks, looking through the material on the new chopper. Their interest had been brought to a high level of intensity and they waited impatiently for the ten minutes to end.

The Filipino AF people left for the day. Truck and the team sat around in the classroom, talking about the past day.

"I've got to say those guys are ready," commented Chuck.

"Ain't that for a fact," agreed Crackers. "They ate up

everything we put out. Those four sergeants assigned to that loading vehicle is as smart as most of them chopper drivers."

"They are an intelligent, well-motivated group—all of 'em. I think this should go pretty smooth," said Truck.

"What say you, Red Dog?" asked The Gooch.

"I don't think we should give these goddamned Filipinos or anybody else this chopper or classified info on how the mother works," growled Red Dog.

"Well, that's an answer," replied The Gooch with a grin.

"Who is duty officer tonight?" asked Truck.

"I am," answered Jumper.

The team had a man on duty every night. He slept in the office in the hangar and would unlock the doors and let in the two interior guards during guard relief. Only members of the team held keys to open the hangar doors. There were two interior guards each night during off-duty hours.

"I think booze is waitin' over at the O Club," said Truck.

They all agreed to that and left to drink a happy hour and then go to the dining room.

Crackers even forgot his basketball that day.

9

Truck got into the rear seat of the sedan provided for him by the Philippine Army. He noticed that the sedan sat heavy on its tires and looked solid. When he saw the reinforced door and thick glass, he knew that he had been provided with a hard-body, or bulletproof, car. He was not sure if this made him feel better or not. This car could stop any rifle bullet that had been developed, but mines, C-4 explosives, and antitank weapons were hell on the paint job. The attempt to kill Crackers and the other two made the Filipinos cautious.

The driver drove out of Clark AFB and into town. When he came to a military post, he turned in and sped through a side gate of Fort Bonifacio, where Headquarters, Army of the Philippines was located.

The driver stopped and the sedan at a designated building, and the army lieutenant sitting in the front seat opened his door before the car came to a full stop. He jumped out and opened the rear door for Truck, holding the salute as the American walked to the door of the building.

73

A general and a colonel were waiting inside the building to greet him. They led Truck to a room with walls covered by maps.

A trim, muscular captain with extremely broad shoulders stood in the room and came to a brace as the men walked in. He wore jump wings and the badge of the Filipino First Scout Ranger Regiment.

General Ruiz introduced himself and the two officers to Truck. "I am General Ruiz, this is Colonel Ramos, and this captain is called Hombros. We are at your service."

Truck agreed with the nom de guerre of "Hombros" for the captain. He also looked the role of an airborne ranger.

"You will have to lead me, gentlemen," replied Truck.

"All right. Ramos is in command of all our special operations and counterinsurgency operations and units. Captain Hombros commands an elite group that is trained in all elements of counterinsurgency. I am their commanding general," Ruiz informed him. "Our existence is unknown to the general public and most of our officials. We must keep our men safe."

Truck nodded his head that he understood.

"I wish to apologize to you and your men for the attempt on their lives," Ramos told Truck.

"You can't protect me and my people all the time any more than my country can," said Truck. "That's just the nature of the beast."

"We will continue to do our best," Ruiz assured him.

"Soon you will be leaving Clark to a secret location to finish your training," said the general. "You will use a base we have in the northwestern part of Tarlac Province. All facilities you need will be present at this secret base we use. Both our air force commandos and our ranger insurgency unit use that base. It is very secure, the first security fence is out of sight or hearing of where you will be training. The primary training area is in a valley that is secured. You will be able to make low-level flights and no one outside the base will see your activities.

"Does that sound reasonable?"

"That's what I'm looking for," admitted Truck.

"We are glad that you and your men are here," Ramos told Truck. "The NPA is getting more and more bold. They are doing their best to disrupt the functions of our government, discredit our president, and turn the people against our renewal of the military bases.

"Some of us know that our internal security is assured as long as the U.S. bases remain in our country. The Communist party knows this as well. That is the reason they are so anxious to get your bases out of here."

"What do you think your government is going to do?" asked Truck. He accepted the cup of hot tea handed him by Hombros.

"If the people have a choice, they would want the U.S. to remain in our country," the general admitted. "We Filipinos know that the we are not a colony of the U.S. That is political jingoism, too.

"We are beginning to learn another fact about these Communist bastards. We believe they will be just as brutal as Pol Pot and his people if they take over our country. They are very brutal and do not care whom they kill or torture. Not many of your people are aware of it, but they have already killed thousands of their own members in purges. We have discovered mass graves with two or three hundred CPF members killed execution style. These people are a fearful bunch. I do not wish them to control the lives of my grandchildren."

"Your country does have a problem," admitted Truck. "I hope we can be of assistance."

"With your helicopters against their antiaircraft weapons,

you will be of assistance," said the general. He put his cup
down on the desk and stood. "We will leave you and the
captain to talk over what you need and to make plans. If you
need anything, let Colonel Ramos know and he will get it
for you.

"Good day, gentlemen."

Colonel Ramos bid both men good day and followed
General Ruiz out of the room.

Truck told Hombros that he would be working directly
with Willie Falloure. He would also work with Bad Bear.

Hombros started to object having to work with a sergeant, but his mind changed as Truck informed him of the
old trooper's background. Truck ended with, "If you want
somebody who knows how to do everything a man needs to
do in a fight—I mean train men, run an operation, call in
arty and air support—you name it, and that old soldier can
and will do it."

"I take your word, sir," Hombros assured him.

The Filipino captain told Truck that he and his men were
already at the camp they were to use. It was one of the
launch sites they used in their counterinsurgency programs
in the northern provinces of Luzon.

Hombros's team would be made up of thirty men,
including him and a lieutenant.

"Did you know Colonel Rowe?" asked Truck.

"Yes, very well, sir. Every time we attack the NPA, I am
extracting payment for what they did to our colonel,"
Hombros said, standing a little straighter.

Truck looked deep into his dark eyes a moment with his
one good eye. Finally he said, "Captain, if you ever need
me for anything, just call."

"Thank you, sir."

Truck turned and walked back out of the building.

The young lieutenant standing by ran to open the door for Truck.

The motor turned and the car jumped forward just as the lieutenant got into the car.

The army sedan drove out of the army post and down the crowded street, weaving in and out of traffic. The colorful jeepneys also dodged in and out of traffic, their drivers firmly believing that most of the highway system in Manila, and the rest of the Philippines, belonged to them.

A red light and traffic stopped the sedan. A white Mercedes sedan pulled up alongside them.

Truck looked at the men in the car with disdain. He knew who they were before the action started. He wished he had a weapon.

Bullets from a submachine gun bounced off the bullet-proof glass and hard body car.

The sedan driver let off the brakes and the car shot out into the intersection, doing some expert driving to get through the traffic with but one fender-bender.

The lieutenant looked back at Truck and was amazed that the old soldier had not even flinched at the bullets bouncing off the windows of the car. The young lieutenant knew that this was an old soldier of many battles and many wars.

"Look, sir," said the lieutenant.

Truck looked back and saw two sedans converge on the white sedan. One had run up alongside the Mercedes and drove it into parked cars. A second sedan pulled in front of the two cars and stopped, blocking all escape. The police-men got out of their sedans, shooting as they walked up to the Mercedes.

"Reckon that oughta put a couple of NPA boys outta business," Truck replied, grinning.

The driver drove into Clark and pulled the sedan up to the

hangar. The lieutenant opened the door and told Truck, "Sir, I will report this incident immediately."

"Thanks," replied Truck. He walked around to the driver's side of the car and looked at where the bullets had hit the bulletproof glass and metal and shattered harmlessly. After a look, he went into the building.

Colonel Yniguez stood in Truck's office, his face red with anger. He told Truck, "We are sure the car belonged to the NPA. The men who tried to assassinate you must have been a team of spies and seen you going into and from Bonifacio. They were probably the same ones who tried to kill your men the other night. The car belonged to members of the NPA. They were some of the so-called Commander Skull's men. The pigs. They murder too many· of our people. We must stop them or this country of mine will fall. It will fall from within."

"That's the reason I don't like to travel among people I work with," said Truck. "I wanna stay covert. Ya don't stay covert by running around with high-profile people."

"That is true," admitted Yniguez. "I am sorry that we subjected you to such an incident."

"I've had worse, Colonel," Truck said, grinning.

"You and your men will soon be moving to a new location."

Truck looked at him.

"No, sir, I do not know where you will be going," the Filipino assured him. "I will learn in due time. I also believe in security measures. The more people who know, the more chance of there being a slip."

"I want three UH-1s, with doorguns for transporting troops. I want a fourth Huey with a gatlin gun mounted on each runner," Truck told the colonel. "I will fly the Huey with the guns and also use it as my C-and-C ship, so I'll need radios for that purpose. We need to keep this training as close to realistic as possible."

"You are using ground troops in connection with air?" asked the Filipino colonel.

"Air or navy can never take or hold a position without ground troops. That's the only way I practice for and the only way I fight a war," Truck told him.

"I'm at your orders, sir," replied Yniguez. He saluted and left.

Truck looked at the woman talking to Jumper Mason. She was a fine-looking Filipino woman in her late thirties to early forties. She was a real beauty. If she had any children, it had not hurt her figure.

She had been in the O Club bar every afternoon at happy-hour time the past week. It seemed to Truck that she had gone out of her way to get close to members of the team. When she found that she could not get anywhere with him, she had moved on to the other members. She was being successful with Jumper. Truck knew that most of the men in the team were old Asian hands and many of them leaned toward Asian women. One such as this woman would be easy to seduce young troopers like Jumper.

Young? thought Truck. Hell! The guy's a Nam vet and been around long enough to be called an old trooper.

"There's too much of this off-the-wall crap been going on. The Communists know we're here. I don't know how, or maybe they're just suspicious of new guys being on the block. But things like that female all of a sudden making an appearance and trying to get next to us guys is a setup. I want a report on that woman," Truck said to Bad Bear.

"I'll get one straight from her," Bad Bear told him. He took another drink from his glass, looking at the woman.

"No, Bear, I don't want anything to come between any

members of the team," said Truck. "Ya start messing with
a woman one of the guys thinks he likes, and it'll drive a
wedge between ya. Let Yniguez's people take a shot at her.
It's their country and their people."

"Yeah, boss, but it's my ass," commented Bad Bear
lightly.

"And I hope you keep it a long time," said Truck.

"*Aho, pah-bee*," Bad Bear thanked Truck.

The men continued drinking into the early evening. But
they did not stay long. They would have a long day
tomorrow and most of them went back to their rooms in the
BOQ.

Jumper stayed at the bar, engrossed by the beautiful
woman who seemed to be attracted to him and him alone.

Truck knew better. This woman was interested and
attracted only by the source where the money and power
came from. Who the source happened to be was his
concern.

Mano sat in the back room of the small café in the poorer
section of Manila. He was a true believer in the ideology of
"power to the people" and was one of them. It was not true
that he was fully one of them, for he was the son of a
wealthy landowner and attorney. He had the same problem
of many young people from a privileged family. He was
ashamed of his family's wealth and felt he had to earn his
place with the poorer people in his society.

Skull was from a high-class, privileged family himself,
but he only went to the places where fine foods and wealthy
people were seen. Mano wondered about him sometimes.
He was sure that when Skull came to power he would rip off
the people like the party members of the Eastern European
countries had been accused of by their opposition. That
thought angered Mano. But Mano had no desire to leave the

side of Skull. Skull was a leader and an organizer who would rise to the top. Mano wanted to be at his side when he reached his destiny.

A man approached his table. Mano motioned him to a chair at his table.

"What news have you?" asked Mano.

"She can learn nothing. They wear uniforms with no name tags or rank. There are no country designations on their uniforms, but we know they're Americans. But no one knows if they are American military or civilians," the man told Mano. "Some think they are CIA. But what they are doing here is a mystery, even to our contacts."

"The man who seems to be their leader was ambushed by one of our teams in an army sedan," replied Mano. "It was unfortunate that he was in one of their hard-body cars."

The other man shrugged his shoulders.

"If these men are here for business, we must find out what that business is. Since no one knows why they are here, then they must indeed be on a very covert operation. But what?" asked Mano, not expecting an answer. He wondered if the Philippine government had learned of their possession of antiaircraft missiles. Such a secret could not be kept forever.

Mano looked at the man and dismissed him with, "That is all for now."

The man left and Mano stood up, motioning for two men to follow him. He had plans to make for the attack on three or four U.S. military bases. That would get the attention of the Filipino people.

Bad Bear walked over to Truck. "Hey, boss, that gal that's been after old Jumper is a widow of an American air force guy. He was a crew member of a Jolly Green Giant that was shot down in 1971. He and the entire crew were

killed. She's been working for the U.S. of A. government
here at Clark since 1970. Her name is Juanita Manley and
she works for maintenance as a secretary for the front
office. She shacks up only with officers—mainly ones who
are on classified business."

"Where'd ya get your info?" asked Truck.

"From the senior sergeant at the O Club. He's been
watching her for a couple of years," replied Bad Bear. "He
don't like her. Thinks she's trouble an' trying to find out too
much about America's business."

"Communist?" asked Truck.

"Don't know. But I'll check with that lieutenant Yniguez
told us to call when we need something," Bad Bear told
him.

"Good. I agree with the sergeant. I don't think I like the
woman, either," growled Truck. He always quickly became
angry with anyone who might interfere in his business.

He walked back into the classroom to listen to Red Dog
give the rest of his class on tactics. They would soon
practice those tactics in actual training exercises.

Colonel Yniguez thanked Truck for calling about Juanita.
The Filipino officer assured Truck that he would look into
the woman's past and present and try to find some info on
her. Hold on, Truck was told.

Two days later, Yniguez called Truck and informed him
that the intelligence service of the Philippine Armed Forces
Military Intelligence Unit assigned to Clark had had the
woman under surveillance for the past two years. She was
suspected of going over to the side of the Huks. Yniguez
asked, "Would you work with us to find out what she is
trying to learn from your man?"

"No, I don't want to get involved with something like

that. We're working on too sensitive a project to get tangled up in something like that. Let the Military Intelligence Unit get the info on her," Truck informed him. "What can you do?"

"As soon as you leave for your new camp, security will bring her in and talk to her for a couple of days," replied Yniguez.

Truck knew that the Filipino security had that much leeway as long as martial law held. He personally did not care what happened to the woman nor was he worried about her civil liberties. He only worried about America's freedom, then everyone else came later. When he was worried about the lives of his men, everything but the Constitution of the United States came second.

He also understood the system that the United States had been working under with the Philippine government in leasing land for military installations. The U.S. had agreed that all military bases would be commanded by a Filipino military officer. With that arrangement, the U.S. military always had direct access to Philippine security services when help was needed.

He called Jumper into his office. The man had to understand where the woman was coming from. He would ask Jumper to go on with the woman like nothing had changed. Truck was sure Jumper would have no problem. He was a professional.

Jumper walked to the door of Bad Bear's room and looked in. Bad Bear ignored Jumper, not because he wanted him to go away, but because he had other things to do. He was getting his gear together for movement to the new location.

"What ya got in that small cedar chest, Bear, if ya don't mind my asking?" Jumper wanted to know.

"Indian stuff," replied Bad Bear.

Crackers walked into the room, handing Bad Bear and Jumper a San Miguel. The three raised the beer in a toast and drank a long pull on their bottles. It had been a long day.

Bad Bear opened the small chest and laid out its contents on his bunk. Then he pulled off his fatigue jacket. His medicine bag was around his neck. He pulled a black Indian "ribbon shirt" over his head. He picked up a string of silver beads of a double strand strung with bone and placed it over his head. The long beads hung from his right shoulder, across his chest, and back to his left hip. He then tied a wide red sash with fringes on each end around his waist and tied it off on his left side. He picked up a head piece made out of otter skin and placed it on his head. Then he put on a pair of moccasins with beautiful beadwork of intricate designs. He told them, "My old aunt is a great craftswoman for our traditional stuff. She made these."

He picked up a fan made of an eagle's wing to hold in his left hand. He picked up a rattle made of a silver saltshaker with his right hand.

He stood, looking exactly what he was. An American Indian warrior.

Bad Bear told them, "I am now dressed for the Kiowa Gourd Dance. Every warrior in the tribe must belong to the Gourd Clan if he is a warrior. In the old days this dance, the Gourd Dance, was held when a war party returned home, and family songs and songs of war were sung. The dance is simple and not as hard as the traditional war dance. It is kept this way so the old warriors and those wounded and disabled in combat can dance the dance.

"This silver beaded thing across my chest is called a bandolier. In the old days men had an arrow quiver slung around their necks. When they got rifles, they used the bandolier. When the U.S. soldiers took away our people's guns and put our people on reservations in Indian territory, we started using these to represent the bandolier.

"This is an otter-skin headgear. We stole the idea from another tribe many years ago. I forget which, but we like it.

"We use what color sash we like. It makes no difference, but a man must wear a sash. I like a red sash and a black shirt.

"In the old days we used gourd rattles. But when the U.S. Army came and we went to fight them, our warriors would overrun an army camp and they would take the salt and pepper shakers from the officers' mess. Our warriors started using silver shakers to make rattles. It was great fun to make something so great from your enemies' belongings. When we shook our rattles, we would mock the soldiers.

"Nowadays we dance the Gourd Dance at powwows. Truck has danced with me. We are brothers. We call a brother *pah-bee*. That means 'brother.' We have been brothers many years. My children call him uncle and his children call me uncle. It is good to have a man of your own choosing as your brother, and not by accident of birth."

"We wondered what all those babas and hohos and other things were," said Jumper.

"*Hatscho* is a greeting when people meet. *Aho* is 'thank you,'" Bad Bear said simply. "Crackers knows much of it."

"I been around those two long enough," admitted Crackers.

The huge Indian had let these two men in for a brief look at him. Just as suddenly he closed them off and placed all of his Indian costume back in its case. He turned his back on them. He was through talking.

His two white team members looked at each other and without a word left the room.

10

Colonel Rufus Holguin showed up at the hangar with a new man. He was Warrant Officer First Class Jackson "Push" Okahara, U.S. Army, of Japanese descent, expert in helicopter maintenance, who had recently become a warrant officer, first grade with a rank designation of WO-1. Jack was a well-built man of average height, with broad shoulders and the trim figure of a man who watched his diet and exercised much of the time. He spent his spare time exercising and could drop down anytime and do over two hundred push-ups, hence his nickname "Push." He was a black belt holder in many of the martial arts as well as combat karate.

The air policeman held the two men at the door until Truck had been notified of their presence. Truck came to the door and led them back to his office.

"Things looking good, Truck?" asked Rufus.

"Yep," was Truck's short answer.

"I heard your need and brought this man. This is WO-1

Jackson Okahara, U.S. Army. He's an expert in maintenance of the AH-64. Jackson, this is Truck Grundy."

"Yes, sir. I've heard of you, Colonel. Anybody that's been around Smoke Bomb Hill has heard of Truck Grundy," said Push, giving Truck a strong handshake.

"You Forces?" asked Truck.

"No, sir, but I worked around the Forces before I got my warrant," Push informed him. "I was a crew chief of a chopper that was working with a team down in Panama when we went in to kick Noriega's ass outta there."

"Welcome to Eagle Attack Team," greeted Truck. "The Filipinos call us Leader Truck, Leader Bad Bear, and so on. What about you?"

"I'll be Leader Push, sir," Push told him.

"The Filipino sergeant in charge of the support vehicle at present is a Sarhento Nino Garcia. I want you to take over the support vehicle and all maintenance," ordered Truck.

"Understood," acknowledged Push.

"You can get with it at anytime," suggested Truck.

The warrant officer looked at the two men, then walked to the door. He opened it, looked at the men standing in front of the classroom, and turned back to Truck. "Now I see why General Olive told me that he was rounding out the color of the team by sending me." Push laughed and walked out of the door.

"He's a good man, Truck. They tell me down at Hood that he can take an AH-64 electrical equipment down and put it back together again while the thing's still in flight," said Rufus, laughing. He accepted the cup of coffee Truck handed him. "He is also qualified to work on most of the computer system and even the mechanics of that damned thing."

"Glad to hear it. We're gonna need a maintenance

capability when we start putting some hours on those things," said Truck.

"You'll get a McDonnell Douglas tech rep when you have bad problems," Rufus informed him.

Truck paused a moment. He had been given a man he had not personally picked or checked out. With a look in Rufus's eyes, he said, "Dan knows I like to pick my own men. I don't appreciate anyone, not even the president of the U.S. picking my men for me."

"The general said you might take this man. He's related to a lieutenant you knew in the Korean War. Dan said he was Ayo Murakami, or something like that," replied Rufus.

"Yep. He was the first platoon leader I had in combat. He was killed in Korea in 1951. Goddamn, he was a good man," remembered Truck. "He was an enlisted man in World War Two with the 442d and got his commission in the reserves. He came back on active duty as a first lieutenant when the Korean War started."

"Push tells me that his father was in the 442d also," Rufus told him. "The cousins served together. Push's father was badly wounded and given a medical discharge from the army."

"We'll try him," said Truck.

"Truck, we think things are going to come to a head here in a few weeks," Rufus told him.

"What do ya mean, 'come to a head'? What do you people know that you're not telling me?" Truck demanded.

"Hold on, Truck. We had some intel, but we didn't know for sure," Rufus told Truck. He walked over to the coffeepot and poured a cup of coffee.

"I ain't to be trusted with sensitive info?" demanded Truck.

"Aw, hell, Truck, it's not that. We think Commander Skull is going to make a move against the established

Philippine government. We don't know when or where. He wants two things: control of the country, and to get the U.S. out of the bases in this country," said Rufus.

"Sure, then the Chinese could move in just like the Russians did in Vietnam," growled Truck. "Question. Is that the reason we're here? Is that why the president allowed us to bring those Apaches over here?"

"To put it bluntly with a Truck answer, 'yep.' We thought we may have to protect our interests," admitted Rufus.

"Then we ain't really gonna give these birds to the Philippine air force?" asked Truck.

"I don't know. There is only an agreement between our two governments to let you come in to the Philippines to train Filipino pilots as a cover for being in the country," Rufus told Truck. He held up a hand to stop Truck. "The general thought I should come over here and let you know what the deal is."

The two men stood, staring at each other. Truck's one eye was as vacant as a clear sky. That worried Rufus and made him a little nervous. He had known Truck since he was a second lieutenant and Truck had been his first commander of an A-team. When Truck's eye got that vacant, untroubled look, things were ready to pop.

"Truck, the Philippine government needs all the help it can get," put in Rufus.

"I realize that," Truck said slowly. "But I'll tell you one goddamned thing, Rufus, and all of ya had better remember this. If you want old Michael 'Truck' Grundy to risk his ass and those of his men in some foreign country, you'd better be up front with me from the start from now on."

"That's what I told them from the start," Rufus put in quickly. He knew Truck Grundy. Truck had spent thirty years in the army and retired as a lieutenant colonel instead of a full colonel because he was subject to tell anyone, general or private, what he thought if crossed.

"They're still looking for Skull's main fort. When they find it, they may want to use the Apaches to blast him loose," Rufus said. "I don't know if they'll call on you or not."

"If that bunch attacks any U.S. facility, I go into action. When they attack the flag, by God, they attack old Truck Grundy," he growled.

Without another word, Truck pulled some papers from a desk drawer and told Rufus, "Let me give you a short briefing ya can take back to Dan."

The two men would socialize later on, hoped Rufus.

Crackers got the basketball from his locker and called the teams together. One team consisted of Eagle Attack Team members, one team of the pilots, one team of the copilots, and one team of the service vehicle team. The two teams that sat in the losers box would sit out the game and play the winner on their time around.

Crackers looked at Push and asked, "Do ya play basketball?"

"Sure," replied the newcomer.

"Good. Any man under sixty years old has to play on the team," Crackers informed him. "See those old geezers over there?" he said, pointing out Red Dog, Chuck, and Truck. "They're the old guys."

Red Dog shot him the finger.

"We've been playing a four-man team against these guys," Jumper informed Push. "We need some help. These Filipino guys ain't American, but they play hell outta basketball."

"Let's play ball," called Bad Bear.

"And watch that damned Indian," The Gooch informed

Push. "Everything he does is for real. There ain't nothing that's a game to him. And a team member is just another player to him. He'll deck ya on your ass if you get in his way like he will anyone else."

Willie walked out onto the floor, his shirt off and a pair of basketball shoes had replaced his jump boots.

"And watch that old black man," Crackers said, pointing to Willie. "He's same age as them three old fogies over there, only he don't know it yet. He'll kill ya. Don't ever play against either of 'em for fun. It ain't."

There was room for two goals in the huge hangar, but they only had one. That did not deter their enthusiasm for the game. It was played in the time-honored tradition of soldier's "combat basketball," which meant everything went and usually did.

The men were their own referees, no one being foolish enough to take on the position by himself. This caused them to spend as much time in arguments as it did in play time. If they had not been members of the same team or allies, there would have been a few killings. Each man would back off just before blood was spilled.

A good time was had by all.

The team was fortunate that they did not venture off Clark Air Force Base those past few days. A team of assassins was waiting for them. Even if the NPA assassins had not killed all of them, they would have broken up the effective-ness of the team.

In the dead of night, when the moon was down and the world was at its darkest hour, the six AH-64s were rolled out of the hangar and prepared for launch. Six Americans would fly the attack helicopters to their new destination and six of the Filipino pilots would fly copilot. The rest of the

Filipino air force personnel would go with the three UH-1 helicopters. Truck would fly the Huey gunship.

Willie and Bo had left a few days earlier in the O-1. Willie wanted to introduce himself to the ranger team that had been formed for their use if necessary, and for training with the attack helicopters.

Push was to leave Clark in a C-130 one hour behind the choppers with the service and rearming vehicle and the Filipino crew.

The U.S. base commander provided security for the stationary trainer that was left behind. No one would be allowed in the building at any time during the team's absence.

Truck watched with a critical eye. This looks like a goddamn circus, he thought. Every move a unit made was like this—confusing to the untrained eye and the uniniti-ated. But to the professional, he could see each man doing his job and moving things along in a coordinated manner. He was glad they were moving to a secret location so they could begin work with the flight crews and the ranger team. He was not one to sit around. Truck Grundy liked action— physical action.

No one saw the Apaches leave Clark. Aircraft were moving in and out at all hours of the day and night from the huge air base. Those on the ground who saw the lights of the choppers and heard the familiar noise of their rotors beating the air were not able to notice any difference in these aircraft and any other. The darkness of the night hid them from view.

An hour later the familiar old C-130 lifted off and flew north. This was not an unusual flight, either.

The team moved without anyone knowing that they had been there, that they had left, or that they even existed.

• • •

Everything was ready when they arrived at the new base. It was small, but well provided for and in an excellent location for secret operations and training.

Bo was glad to have company. He had been having a hard time drying out and Bad Bear had been no help. Bad Bear could live without anyone around. And he had no sympathy for Bo. Bo felt the Indian was inhuman.

11

They spent most of their nights training, for Truck believed in night operations. He and the others had relearned the importance of night-operations fighting against the Viet Cong and North Vietnamese Army during the Vietnam War.

The Filipino soldiers were amazed at the capabilities of the Apache. The machines were more devastating than the men had been led to believe. The Filipinos wondered if by some miracle the Americans would leave them such an aircraft for their air force.

Truck was satisfied with the training area they had. The Filipino commander of the base provided them with a number of targets to use and gave them good support. It was a satisfying arrangement.

The men worked in the heat of summer, the Americans staying wet from sweat most of the time.

Bad Bear and Willie found while training in the bush that the Philippines was like any other place in the southeastern part of Asia and the Pacific. The bush was triple-canopied jungle, hot and humid and home to pythons, bamboo vipers, cobras, wild hogs, wild water buffaloes, leeches, and billions of mosquitoes.

Professional soldiers did not worry about such things as a few discomforts. They always had their eye on higher things and the flag. And the love of their life—war.

When they were off from the night training, they gathered in the small officers' bar and mess in the Filipino special operations complex. A few women had been invited to the club before the Americans arrived, but Truck had demanded that all non-military personnel be kept off the base. Besides, if they had come on base, these were local women from a small community and Truck would not allow any of his men to violate his orders against fraternizing with local women. Not even if they were local whores. Americans had too much money to throw around, and most host nations' citizens hated them for it.

The Filipinos grumbled about their women being banned from the post, but they had been given orders that no one was to know about the strange helicopters that were now on post.

They shrugged their shoulders.

Crackers stood with his basketball. The first priority after getting settled and fulfilling all military duties was for him to put up his basketball hoop. He asked Push, "Ya wana play a little one-on-one?"

"Yeah, I'll play with ya," replied Push.

"Watch it, Jap, he cheats," called Gooch.

"Oh, were we to play by rules?" Push asked innocently with a grin.

"Uh-oh. I think Crackers done got himself an opponent that'll stick with him," laughed Jumper.

"Let's watch the blood fly," suggested Gooch.

The game was a hot one and ended with Crackers owing Push a case of beer. The beer was to be San Miguel, and none of that American stuff.

Bad Bear, Crackers, Jumper, and The Gooch sat drinking beer with the new team member, Push.

"Hey, where did a guy of Japanese ancestry get a first name like Jackson, even if he is American?" asked Crackers.

"My dad was in the 442d during World War II. One of his platoon leaders was a guy called Jackson. None of the Japanese could be officers. When they were fighting in Italy, my father was badly wounded. Some of the guys he was with were cut off from the rest of the platoon and company. This guy, Lieutenant Jackson, dragged my father back to the American lines while under heavy fire, fighting all the way. Dad said Jackson got hit twice, but he wouldn't let my dad go," Push paused, remembering his father's story. "He got Dad back to lines when an artillery round came in. Jackson fell down on top of my dad to shield him from the explosion. The round killed the lieutenant and wounded my father even worse than he already was.

"After the war, when he got married, he said he was gonna name his first kid after that lieutenant. That was me, and I'm proud of the name."

"Goddamn, I don't blame ya," put in The Gooch. "I'd even take the name of Okahara for something like that."

"Hell, a man'd give his life for my ole man, I'd take Shit as a good name," Crackers said honestly.

Truck passed the table on his way out of the small club. He told them, "Boys, we're gonna have a long day tomorrow. Right up to about twenty-three hundred hours."

The tall man continued on out the door without pausing.

"We do what he says?" asked Push.

"What do you think?" asked Jumper, downing his beer.

"From what my dad's cousin told me about the colonel, I don't think I want any more beer tonight," replied Push, getting up and leaving.

The other men followed.

Colonel Ramos, commander of the counterinsurgency forces, came to the camp. He called Truck, Captain Hombros of the First Scout Ranger team, and Captain Castello, leader of the helicopter pilots, to a meeting. Lieutenant Colonel Peña Romeros, commanding officer of the camp, was also present.

"Our intelligence service has learned that Commander Skull is up to something. The only information they have at present is that whatever it will be, it will be soon, it will be drastic, and it will upset the entire government of the Philippines," Ramos told the men. "This man is capable of anything. He will do anything to bring this government and country to its knees. With the capabilities we have with these Apaches, we must be ready to hit Skull's fort as soon as it's located."

"We think we know where it is located," said Peña. "We have lost two good men, killed, trying to find that place. This man is smart, this Communist who calls himself Skull. He has four of five places that are decoys. We have found four of them."

"You must keep up your work. The IS will give you all the intelligence they have or they receive on Skull and his people," stated Ramos.

"I hope that is so. We have gotten nothing from them so far," growled Peña.

"When that fort is located, you are directed to use all force you need to neutralize that place," ordered Ramos. "If you can't capture that bastard Skull, make sure you kill him. We don't want that man to escape. He is nothing but trouble and will be trouble as long as he lives."

"It will be done," Peña assured him.

Ramos looked at Truck and said, "The training, is it going well?"

"Very well. Bad Bear, the Indian, has been working with Hombros and Willie," Truck told him.

"He teaches us the fine art of going into safe houses. We needed this training," admitted Hombros.

"Bad Bear and I both were part of the Phoenix Program in Vietnam," said Truck. That statement answered all questions for these professional soldiers.

"Good. I think all of your training will be needed," said Ramos. He stood, shook hands with the men, and departed.

The four men walked to the aircraft and watched it take off with the army colonel.

"I will alert the entire camp for possible action," Peña told the three men. "All leaves and passes will be canceled, and the women will go only to the house provided for them. An escort will take them directly to the house and back to the main gate. They will not be allowed to wander the camp or clubs. The men can go to see the girls for thirty minutes at a time only."

"Yes, Colonel, it will be done," the two captains agreed.

"Hell. Thirty minutes would be enough for me anytime," The Gooch said under his breath.

"Shit. Two hunches and you're through," put in Crackers.

Truck smiled. He did not like Peña letting the girls come in, but it would be dark and they would not see the choppers. Men's needs had to be taken care of.

Mano Garcia made the long trip to the fort to see Skull. He had hoped he would be able to make his plans and then execute his offensives without further talks with Skull. He was tired of Skull. He was tired of the mountains and the jungle. He was tired of playing the guerrilla.

He walked into the bunker where Skull sat waiting at a table. He gave an offhanded salute and joined Skull at the table.

"Your trip was well?" asked Skull.

"It was okay," replied Mano. I shouldn't have had to make this trip, he growled in his mind.

"I wanted to see you face-to-face. We are too close to our goals to have our communications intercepted," Skull told Mano.

At least he has a reason for pulling me out of the city and onto this damned mountain, thought Mano.

"We must speed up our plans. We must go as soon as possible," explained Skull.

"No! We cannot. I have more people to get into place. I have more to do if we want this plan to be successful," exclaimed Mano.

"I will go now. I have received word that those ten Americans have pulled out of Clark and disappeared. You yourself sent word that the woman had also disappeared. If that is so, she must have become suspect and is being held incommunicado," said Skull. "I don't know why these Americans were sent here, but it is for no good reason except to find and attack us."

This caused Mano to pause. Things were becoming complicated ever since "Gringo" Honasan's failed coup attempts. The president and the military were getting nervous, wondering what was going to happen next. And of course there was the United States to worry about. They held their ability to retain their military bases in the Philippines as one of their top foreign-affairs matters. They would do anything and everything to get the Filipino people and government to back extension of those bases.

"I will give the Philippine government something to keep it busy while you plan and make your attacks on the U.S. military bases," Skull told Mano with a grin.

"What do you plan to do?" asked Mano.

"Take a hostage," grinned Skull. "One close to the president. It will have the government and military out looking for something they cannot find while you make your move. It will be a great diversion."

"I hope it works. We need something to keep the military off balance while we move into place," agreed Mano. "With a hostage situation facing the government, it will keep both the Military Intelligence Service and the National Intelligence and Security Authority occupied. That will give us some room to maneuver and get our people in place."

"Good. It will be done. Three days and the hostages will be taken. Five days from now our master plan will be executed. We will conquer these tyrants while they look for miracles to return their hostages," laughed Skull. Skull called for rum. It was brought and he poured two glasses full and handed one to Mano. "To the power of the people!"

They drank to the toast.

The curtain of the door was left open, indicating that the meeting between the two men had ended.

A young woman eased into the room and stood to one side of the door next to the wall. She looked at Mano hungrily. She had been without her man too long.

Skull saw her. Laughing, he said, "You have other business for now, my friend. Finish your other business and be off to do our people's work."

Mano finished the glass and stood. He smiled and walked to where the woman stood. He asked, "You have missed me?"

"Yes," she replied quietly.

He planned to fill the void she felt.

• • •

Truck sat at the small table he used as a desk. He took a sip of bourbon and thought of the progress he and the team had made since they came to the Philippines. He was not agreeable to leaving any Apaches behind for the Filipinos, but if they ever had a need for these attack choppers, they had a small core of young pilots who had been trained for their use.

He knew now that they had been sent to this camp to be close to Skull's fort. It was not known where the fort was located, but it would be found. The Philippine government was making an extra effort to locate Skull's stronghold after it was learned that he now had antiaircraft weapons. He had become a serious threat since he had some control of the air. It was fortunate that he had learned Willie was in Manila. With both Willie and Bad Bear working with the rangers, the Filipinos would learn twice as fast and twice as much. Each man had their own expertise to give the ranger team.

Chuck knocked on the door and entered the room.

Truck offered him a drink, which Chuck turned down.

"Think action's ready to begin?" asked Chuck.

"Something is up," admitted Truck.

"I think we're ready for whatever comes," said Chuck.

"Yep," agreed Truck. "Let shit hit the fan, I'm ready."

"Me, too. This'll be my last one," smiled Chuck, not sure he was glad of the fact. He knew he would miss the service, the camaraderie of men such as these he worked with, and the action. All of his friends who had already retired wanted back on active duty. Truck had told him that he would quickly find that no one was in charge once he got into civilian life. But at least he would have time with the family before the last of his kids left. Sea time had eaten away a lot of his fatherhood period. Maybe he could be at home with Frances and make up for some of the lost husbandhood time.

"I think I'll write a letter to Fran and hit the sack," said Chuck.

"Yeah, I owe Linn a letter. Reckon now's a good time to do my fatherly duty," returned Truck. He noticed that men tend to write home to loved ones when it looked like hot lead was about to start flying. Well, I've seen plenty of it, he mused.

"Goddamn it, Bear, stop throwing that fuckin' knife!" bawled Jumper. "You'd scare piss out of a fence post with that thing!"

There was no response from Bad Bear.

Truck smiled. Bear must have thrown his knife close to someone who came into his room. It was good for practice, but hell on walls—and friends' nerves.

12

Joe Ybarra gave his wife a quick kiss and ushered his two daughters and son to the front door. He was running late and had to get to the Presidential Palace. He would drop the children off at school on his way to work.

Ybarra was an important confidant and personal adviser to the president. He was good with "problem" people and organizations. The president trusted him completely to do his job and protect both her and their country.

He had spent most of last night discussing the treaty for continued U.S. base leases in the Philippines with concerned individuals. Long, heated discussions had been held with many groups that were on both sides of the issue.

The kids were finally herded into the car.

God! I'm glad I don't have this duty every morning, he laughed to himself. He drove out of the gate and onto the busy street.

Three cars sat on the side of the street two blocks away. The men in these automobiles knew this man's habits and were anticipating them. He was late this morning, but he always traveled this route.

When Ybarra's car passed the three cars, they pulled into the street and followed for another block. The leader noticed that this morning the Ybarra children were in the car. He was pleased. Children were worth more than the adult. Kidnapping the children may concern Commander Skull, but they were ordered to get Ybarra this morning. The order would be accomplished.

Juan Serna motioned the driver to pull in front of Ybarra. A second car pulled to the side of Ybarra's car, and with a car in front, on the driver's side, and to the rear, the government official was effectively blocked off.

Ybarra stopped the car when his wheels hit the curb.

Armed men jumped out of the three cars and jerked Ybarra and his three children out of their car. The children were put in one car, the two girls screaming and kicking. Ybarra was placed in another car. The three automobiles speeded off, joining the throng of vehicles in the busy morning rush. The kidnapping was done quickly and expertly.

The leader of the armed group hit Ybarra sharply in the mouth. "Do not speak, capitalist pig. You are now a prisoner of the New People's Army."

"My children . . . ," Ybarra started.

The leader laughed. "They will become good Communists." After a pause, he said brutally, "That is, if they live."

The screams of the two girls and the pleading voice of the boy were not heard over the noisy traffic.

Lieutenant Colonel Peña Romeros called Truck, Hombros, and Castello to a meeting. He met them in the war room of the operations section. Both the intelligence and operations officers stood by in case their commander needed them. Otherwise there were no other people in the room.

Peña pointed to an aerial photo on an A-frame marked Top Secret and then to a spot on a map. "This picture was taken at this location. We believe this to be Commander Skull's base camp and headquarters—his stronghold, or fort, as they call them. It looks like a normal hunting and woodsman camp. You can see buildings in the clearings," he said, pointing them out in the picture. "But back under the canopies of the trees, we find at the angle this picture was taken structures that look like long bunkers. If you look closer, there seem to be trenches running between these mounds. They are well camouflaged."

Peña took down the picture and displayed another one on the A-frame. "After that first picture, we went back for another shot. See these? It appears that there are more bunkers. And, indeed, there are a few trenches that show up more clearly. The man who designed this fort and the other ones knows about aerial photography."

The colonel straightened up and looked at the three men. "This is the area my scouts believed to be the location of Skull's main fort. From the size of these structures, these pictures confirm their suspicions."

Truck got up from his chair and walked to the picture for a closer look. "Do you have some photos of villages in the area taken at the same altitude?"

"Yes," replied Peña. He motioned the S-2 to bring out the photos.

The photos were produced and Truck stood studying them in detail. He had spent a few hours in classes and actually used photo analysis in combat situations. It was more a case of "work at it" than an art. After a moment, he told the men, "Look at the difference in these structures at the site of Skull's fort and the other structures in the region.

These buildings at the fort are much larger, and some are of a different design. There is no doubt in my old feeble military mind, that these buildings have the antiaircraft weapons."

The Filipino officers came forward and looked at the aerial photos.

Peña picked up a large magnifying glass and looked at the structures in a number of photos. "Yes, my friend, you are right," he said appreciatively. "There is a definite difference in their size and in some cases, even their design."

Peña looked at Hombros and asked "Do you think a patrol can get close enough to check this fort out?"

"Yes," he answered. "It will take a couple of days, but it will be done."

"Good. Then I order it," Peña told him.

Hombros took down the proper map coordinates and asked for a smaller aerial photograph. He took the map and photo and departed, ready to plan the patrol.

"Gentlemen, we have work to do," said Peña.

The other men saluted and left, leaving Truck and Peña in the room.

Truck told Peña, "We have trained your pilots, but I am not sure that they will be able to handle such a mission as this. They haven't had enough training."

"If we receive orders from Quezon City, what will you do?" asked Peña.

"We'll attack that damned fort. My men and I will fly the choppers. The Filipino pilots will ride copilot. I won't let inexperienced men take those birds up for a flight," Truck told him bluntly.

"We of the Philippines will gratefully accept your help. All of your men are more experienced at this business than our people, but I am sure that we will become more and more able to fight this kind of war as time goes on," replied

Peña. "We have been fighting the Huks and Moros in a piecemeal fashion. It has not worked. It never will work. So we must and will change."

"I wish my country could change as well. About the time we military men get our act down pat and ready to play by the proper rules, our government changes the rules on us," growled Truck. "We're gonna pay some of these days, or change our act also."

"The problems of politicians running the wars," said Peña with a smile.

"Yeah," agreed Truck. "I gotta get with it, Peña. We've got a lot to do to get those birds ready."

"I don't think I'd better go on this patrol," Willie told the men as they were getting ready. "I done passed the age to get into shape quickly, and we only been at this a couple of weeks now. And I've been sitting on my ass sucking up beer for the past few years. Get in shape and I'll run y'all's dried-up little butts in the ground. Right now, I'll let you younger men do the job until I get back in shape."

"Since I'm not only younger than you are, by about forty years, and not as shot up as you were in Nam, I'm gonna make this trip," said Bad Bear. "I've missed the excitement of physical contact."

Hombros nodded and then told them, "Okay, then it's four men. You, Bad Bear, Lieutenant Gutierrez, and Sergeants Fagan and Chapa will go. A chopper will take you to a dropoff point and you will go by foot the rest of the way. We want only intel, not bodies. Do not let them know you have been there. If you must kill a man, hide him so he will not be found. There will be a pickup point when you call."

"I've got to go get ready," said Bad Bear, and left.

"Ya got a good man going with you, Lieutenant," Willie told Gutierrez.

"This I already know," agreed the lieutenant.

The men left the briefing to get ready for the night patrol.

Bad Bear looked down at his medicine bag and nodded his head. It was good. He took out the stainless-steel mirror he used for applying his camouflage and went about painting himself with deliberate designs. He was applying warrior designs, because he was going to do warrior things. He was going in harms way.

When the war paint was finished, he took a black rag, rolled it to the proper width, and tied it around his head for a sweatband. He put on his web gear with pistol, knife, ammo pouches, and two water canteens. All loose equipment was tied or taped down, ranger style. He pulled the knife out of its sheath and gave an unnecessary check of its sharpness. He snapped a small medical pouch to his gear. The patrol was going where no local hospitals were in operation. When all of that was done, he picked up his M-16 and walked out of the barracks the Americans used.

Gutierrez was waiting with his men. They had also tied down all equipment and camouflaged their faces. They were combat ready.

Truck walked up to the men. "We want intel, not bodies. If they find out we've been snooping around their home base, they may change things around to give us a reception we ain't looking for. Or worse still, they just may up and move from that place. Then we'd have to start all over again."

Gutierrez looked at the old soldier and said, "Yes, sir. We will do our best to complete our mission."

Bad Bear looked at Truck in the pale light. "Okay, boss. We'll be good little soldiers."

"*Aho, pah-bee*. That makes me feel a hell of a lot better," Truck said dryly.

The whine of a UH-1 helicopter winding up was heard.

Bad Bear slapped Truck on the shoulder as he passed, and the one-eyed Texan said, "I wish I was still in good enough shape to be going with you."

"Boss, everybody here knows you got more combat time and been on more missions than any of us. So give us young studs a chance," Bad Bear told him as he passed on in the dark.

"Go well, *pah-bee*," Truck called after him. Truck knew that if anyone could make the trip back alive, Cliff Sate-Zalebay was probably that person.

Bad Bear jumped off the UH-1 and was followed by the three Filipino soldiers. Bad Bear ran to the tree line and quickly looked at his wrist compass in the failing light.

Gutierrez pulled out his map case and oriented it with the direction Bad Bear gave him as compass, or magnetic, north. The two men looked the map over as the other two soldiers kept a lookout. They not only watched for NPA but also for civilians passing through the area who could give them away.

When their route of march had been determined, Bad Bear led off.

Gutierrez and his two men were from the mountains of Luzon and knew the mountains well. But the lieutenant had learned while working with the two Americans that this big one was an expert at tracking and finding his way in the bush. The Kiowa had proved to the Filipino the tales he had heard about the American Indian.

Bad Bear figured from the distance on the map that climbing up a mountain and the thickness of the forest would put them at the NPA fort at around 0400 hours. That meant they would have to get in and out quickly. They were moving up the southwest side of the mountain, so the light of the new sun would not hit them directly. They could keep in the shadows if necessary. He only hoped they could get in and out before it was light enough to have to hide in the shadows.

If they failed to get out of the area before the sun came up, they would have to remain in place under leaves, brush, or whatever covering they could find. He remembered that on one of the early raids his team had made into Laos near the Ho Chi Minh Trail, they had been caught in daylight near a group of trail workers that decided to rest for the remainder of the day. His team had spent the entire day caught among them, covered with dirt and leaves, until night came and they could move under darkness.

Bad Bear signaled for a halt. He crawled back to the three men. He whispered, "I have made contact. An exterior guard has been reached."

The four men crawled forward quietly. When Bad Bear stopped, the other men crawled up alongside him. It was dark on the jungle floor.

Gutierrez took out his night light device and looked toward the direction Bad Bear pointed him. He swept the area and finally saw the movement of a man. The man was dressed in an NPA bush uniform.

Bad Bear motioned for them to follow him around the sentinel.

The men passed the exterior guard and moved up the hill to the outer perimeter of the fort.

Bad Bear found trip wires for illumination rounds, noise makers, and other devices, but he did not run into wire entanglements. A defense wire-fence entanglement would show up in aerial photos.

An interior guard was spotted and stood in the way of their movement to the structure that loomed ahead of them.

The four men stopped.

Bad Bear handed his rifle to one of the men and pulled out his huge bowie-type knife. He crawled forward until he reached open ground. He stood up and walked on "feet with eyes" to the guard. He slipped a powerful arm around the neck of the guard and stuck the knife in his back. He shoved the handle to the right and jerked it quickly back in the other direction. The movement destroyed the man's kidneys and lower part of his heart. He was dead before Bad Bear lowered him to the ground.

The Kiowa slung the guard's rifle around his shoulder, picked the man up, and carried him back to where the other men waited. After laying the man on the ground, he motioned Gutierrez to follow. The other two men remained on guard.

The two men crept to the building. Inside they heard a man snoring lightly. Bad Bear eased the curtain of the door to one side and in the flickering of a small oil lamp he saw a Soviet-built ZPU-4 14.5mm heavy antiaircraft machine gun. The gun had quad barrels and was mounted on a four-wheel trailer. The small caliber would not do much harm to the Apaches, but they would bring death and destruction to UH-1s and other aircraft.

Off to their right stood another building. The two men crept up to it and peered inside. It was pitch black inside.

Bad Bear held up a hand for Gutierrez to hold in place. He eased inside and stood a moment. His heart did not increase its beat out of fright. Hell, this was fun! There was no one inside. He pulled out his small flashlight and flicked it on long enough to see the weapon. It was an old Soviet M1939 37mm antiaircraft gun mounted on a four-wheel trailer. He had also seen those in Vietnam. Now, that one would knock an Apache out of the air.

He wondered how these people had gotten these things up the mountain without anyone seeing them? That was a foolish thought. Men can do just about anything when it came to killing each other.

A quick look and the two men made their way back to the other two soldiers.

"Go," Gutierrez ordered quietly.

One of the men picked up the guard's rifle and Bad Bear picked up the enemy soldier and slung him over his shoulder. The four men walked quietly back down the mountain. They were well away from the outer perimeter before the sun came up.

When they reached a shallow gully with the side walls of loose and crumbling dirt and rocks, they placed the man and his weapon at the bottom of the small cliff and pushed dirt on top of him. It was doubtful if he would be found for a number of days or even weeks.

"We've got a report for the colonel," said Bad Bear.

"Yes, it is a good one," said Gutierrez. He had lost men and wasted enough time trying to find Skull's fort. Now the traitor to his country would be paid back for all the trouble and death he had caused.

When the four-man patrol reached their pickup point, Gutierrez called in the UH-1 pickup chopper. They had been in Skull's stronghold, and the Communist leader was not even aware of it. But soon he would be aware that the secrecy of his hideout had been compromised.

It was late morning.

13

General Ruiz called Colonel Ramos into his office. The general told Ramos, "The president is furious about the abduction of Ybarra and his children. You can understand why. Here this lady has been trying to take our country from a corrupt despotic rule to one that is democratic and ruled by the people. What has happened since she came to office? There have been disparaging remarks by members of her own administration, numerous coup attempts, trouble from the CPP and from the Moros, and now her trusted adviser is abducted. And not alone. They took his children also, the pigs.

"The president insists that we attack Skull's fort as soon as it is located. The National Bureau of Investigation is working with our Intelligence Service to track down the abductors of Ybarra and his children. They are believed to still be in the city.

"But that's the problem for the NBI and IS. Our main

efforts are to locate and destroy Skull's fort and his military capability."

"Peña and his men are getting ready to make an assault as soon as the main fort is located. They think they have his location pinpointed. They now have a patrol out to confirm its location. The patrol left late this afternoon and it is hoped they will return sometime tomorrow," Ramos told Ruiz. "The Americans are willing, able, and ready to fly the Apache helicopters against Skull. Peña told me that Truck is ready to make the Communists pay for killing his friend, the late Colonel Rowe. These Americans wish to take vengeance, even though their country is not willing to commit itself to such an action."

"A country must be willing to protect and seek justice for the men they send out into the world to do its business," growled Ramos.

"But we are considered a third-world country in the community of nations and do not have to act as sophisticated as the Americans and other great world powers," answered Ramos, smiling.

"Then here's hoping that we never become a sophisticated nation," said General Ruiz. "When my men hurt, I want to get revenge for them. An eye for an eye, as it were."

"We will do our job in the field, General. Now, if these civilian types will do theirs and find Ybarra and his children, we will beat this Skull and his Communist bandits," Ramos assured his commander. "When do we get orders to attack? As soon as the location of Skull's fort is confirmed?"

"I'm not sure, but it should be soon. We must at least try to deal with Skull for the return of Ybarra and his children. Of course, we cannot treat with terrorists and kidnappers. But we must do what we must do," the general told him.

"If we can destroy Skull's military operation in his own playground, we have a chance of stopping the CPP dead in their tracks. At least we can get some control," replied Ramos.

"Yes, it is best to keep the Communists reduced to guerrilla activities than letting them build up to an active army-size organization," replied Ruiz.

"I have much work, General." Ramos saluted and left the office.

After Colonel Ramos departed, General Ruiz picked up the telephone and told the party on the other end, "Our operation in the mountains is going as planned. Inform the president that all is under control on our end."

He hung up the telephone and smiled. He would see that this so-called people's army was put in its place like those renegade army officers who wanted to destroy the democratic republic of his country. He took great pride in his ability to separate his duties as a professional soldier from those of elected officials of his people. He was a soldier, not a politician.

Juan Serna walked into the room that held Joe Ybarra. He looked at the man and laughed. "We have told the government that we take ten million dollars for you. If the kids are thrown in, we take ten million more."

"You pig! Where are my children?" demanded Ybarra.

Serna hit Ybarra in the stomach. The smaller man eased himself onto the floor.

Serna growled, "You wealthy capitalist dog, don't make demands of me. You don't have the power of the almighty government standing by you now. It's just me and you, on equal grounds."

This man considered Ybarra, under armed guard of henchmen, to be on an equal footing. He did not have the mental capability to figure the difference or the proper use of power. He was only muscle power for the movement and would go where a greater power bid him go.

Serna continued, "We will also demand that our country kick the capitalistic Americans out of our country and take back the military bases they've held so long. They are defiling Philippine sovereignty and territory by their presence."

"It will be better under Chinese domination, is that it, you fool?" Ybarra shot back.

Serna kicked him for his outburst. He told the captive, "You should not worry. You will not care." He gave a burst of laughter. "You will not care about anything."

"My children, they have nothing to do with this!" screamed Ybarra. "They are innocent of all this. They are babies."

"Children are guilty of their father's sins," growled Serna, then he gave an evil grin. "Your little girls have good pussy, man. Your son must be teaching them right."

Ybarra screamed out in agony. "Oh, God, no! Don't let this be happening!"

"Don't pray to God, pig. Pray to me, *Aguerrido*. I got the gun. And I got your little girls," laughed Serna. He left the room, Ybarra's screams following him down the hall.

Mano Garcia sat drinking his cold beer. He had issued orders. Now all he could do was wait. Wait and wonder if he had done the right thing. Wait and wonder if he should have argued more strongly against attacking the U.S. military targets at this time. Skull insisted that if they struck the Americans and made it seem that they were vulnerable, then the people would fall in behind the NPA. He had also said his propagandist had been at work and was swaying the people. But Mano was worried. He knew his people. The

Filipino people would follow a strong leader and a strong cause. But they would also be led by what they thought was in the best interest of their country. After the many failed coup attempts by military renegades and the outlawry of the Huks the past couple of years, added to the disturbances caused by the Moros, he was not sure if the people of the Philippines were ready for men outside an elected government to rule them.

A woman came into the room and walked over to him. She stood at his back, rubbing his tight neck and shoulder muscles. She was not the woman he had seen at camp. That had been his "field wife." This woman was a city girl. She would not stay with him or any man in the bush. She was his "city mistress." His "church wife" had not learned of either woman, although she suspected him of infidelity. He was not concerned. His wife was a good Catholic, not he. He was a Communist and did not have any of the inhibitions of papacy trappings.

"Mano, I am lonesome and want to go to bed," she whispered in his ear.

Her exploring tongue sent shivers through him and drew his crotch tight. He informed her, "You're not alone. I'm in the house."

"I know, but I want you in bed," she purred.

"I have business."

"You always have business," she complained. She flounced off to the other side of the room. "I don't know why I don't get me another man. One who will take care of my needs more often."

"Because no one man could take care of your needs—and have any strength left," he said with a smile. "And, I am one of the few men you have met who can take care of some of those needs. More so than any man you have met before."

"I know, Mano, I know. But I need you now, not tomorrow or in the morning. I need you now," she moaned.

"If you had me now, you would still need me in the morning," he laughed. He sat a moment, looking at her beauty. If he was going to take her, he had better do it now. He would have no time in the next few days. By the dawn's early light, things in the Philippines would change forever.

Mano stood up. "All right, lead me to your lair."

She squealed happily and ran out of the door. He followed, pulling off his shirt as he walked to the bedroom. She was undressed and waiting for him as he closed the door.

The men in the next room heard her squeal and smiled. Their leader was going to be satisfied tonight. They knew he would not satisfy the woman. No ten men could satisfy that one. Most of them had tried.

The men played a game of basketball, the Filipino copilots winning over the Eagle Attack Team. They were a group of young men in excellent physical shape.

Crackers stood, tears in his eyes and a look of devastation on his face. He stammered in mock sorrow and exasperation, "I can't believe it! My men, my friends let a bunch of young, upstart Filipinos beat the living hell outta us! We—us Americans who invented this game. They beat us every goddamned time they play us. I'm gonna get me another team!"

The young Philippine air force men stood grinning broadly, enjoying the show Crackers was putting on.

"Go on, git! Don't come near my basketball no more," cried Crackers.

This brought boos from all of the Filipinos.

The Gooch brought out the case of San Miguel beer to pay the debt and served the winners of the ball game. He looked at the other Filipino men standing around watching everyone drink beer and went back inside the barracks used by the Americans. He came out with another case and all had beer at the expense of the Americans, the inventors of basketball.

Truck and Peña left the men and walked back toward the mess hall.

"You think we're gonna have orders to attack the forts now that one of the president's men has been captured?" asked Truck.

"I am sure of it," answered Peña. "They will be more than willing if we confirm the location of Skull's main fort."

"We'll have the men hold down on their drinking tonight. If we go, it could be at any time," said Truck.

"The high command wants us to get rid of Skull and his fort. Wipe it clear off the map of the Philippines with him in it," Peña informed him.

"I suggest we tell Hombros and Willie to make sure Skull is killed in the action. Your president tried to be conciliatory to that guy Gringo, and look what happened," said Truck. "He escaped from his imprisonment and caused the deaths of a lot of your countrymen."

"Yes, that is correct. We should not allow this to happen again," agreed Peña. "A dead Skull is only a martyr, not a leader, because dead men can't lead."

"I agree with that," said Truck.

"We also captured that Communist Jose Maria Sison in 1977. When Aquino came to power, she thought it would be a conciliatory gesture and the Communists would become good boys if she freed him," complained Peña. "Our president is learning a lesson that no one needs to learn. That there are some people in this world who answer only to the gun and power."

"That's for a fact," agreed Truck. "I'm hungry."

"Me, too. Eating is not as good as whiskey or a woman, but food is a good substitute for many things for a soldier," said Peña, laughing, not believing a thing he said.

Chuck caught up with Truck and Peña. "Everything and everyone's ready to go. All we're waiting on now is the word."

"It might come right soon," Truck informed him.

The three of them walked into the mess. Red Dog was already sitting at a table eating his nightly steak. A bottle of scotch was on the table.

Truck said to hell with the old pilot's idiosyncrasies and walked over to Red Dog's table. They had things to talk about and he talked when he got good and ready.

The three men pulled out chairs and sat down.

Red Dog looked up with a sour look and asked, "What ya need?"

"Are you ready?" asked Truck. "And do you need anything?"

"I'm ready, and if I'd needed anything, I'd a asked," said Red Dog in between bites.

"How's that observer working out with Bo?" asked Truck.

The girl came and served the men their meals. She was one of the sergeant's wives.

"Okay. He's been doing some good spotting with that night scope," Red Dog informed him. "Bo says he can give us targets before daylight hits, if we need 'em."

"Good. You know me; I like night fighting," said Truck.

"I like fightin' any goddamn time, except when I'm eating," put in Red Dog.

Jumper walked up to their table.

"Well, goddamn, who the hell else is coming in?" asked Red Dog disgustedly.

"Not me, Red Dog. I ain't got that many guts," Jumper

grinned. "Truck, Crackers said the choppers are ready. He and Push checked out everything. You call, we'll haul."

"If we have to go up, I'll fly that Huey. Chuck'll be in command of the attack force," Truck informed them. "I want Push to be standing by for Apaches to come in in pairs. I know he'll be pushed for time, but it's gonna work that way.

"We don't know for sure when the high command'll give us the word to go. Until then, we're on standby, red alert, until something does happen. Everyone conduct themselves accordingly."

"We gotcha, Colonel," replied Jumper, and left to join the other men.

Men and women sat and waited outside of the Clark U.S. Air Force Base, Subic Bay U.S. Naval Base, Cubi Point U.S. Naval Station and U.S. Naval Communications Station, both in Zambales Province, and Wallace U.S. Air Station in La Union Province. Most of the bases had no fences on the outer edges, trusting in patrolling Filipino army and marines. Since U.S. Army Colonel Rowe had been assassinated, the Americans had increased the number of patrols by their own units' security people. They would hit their heaviest resistance when they neared the airfields, ship docks, and other facilities.

These people who waited were men and women of the New People's Army. They waited with mortars, rockets and small arms to do their duty against the imperialist Americans. They were going to rid their country of the paternalistic Americans who had held domination over their country for all these years.

They waited for the signal. Then they would attack. Little or no thought was given to the likelihood that none or few of them would survive this attack alive. When the heroic blood of ideology flowed hot and strong, what was the concern of the loss of a few lives to get what you wanted?

Skull waited with his favorite young boy in his bed. It did not matter to him if it was a woman or a man in his bed. Just as long as he was not alone in the dark. Nighttime was always a foreboding time for Skull. The family's children's nurse or one of the house maids had slept in his bed since the day his father brought him and his mother home from the hospital six days after his birth. He never slept with a middle-aged woman. He always demanded a younger woman to keep the night things away from his bed. He had learned that a freedom fighter who lived in the bush did not always have a woman handy. He compromised. Mano thought he was sick.

Skull smiled. Soon he would be in Manila or Quezon City, where he would never run short of women or young boys.

He also waited.

14

The order was given over the radio. The attack was on.

"Hey, did ya hear that?" a U.S. Navy radio operator at the naval communications station asked.

"What's that?" a sleepy chief radio operator asked.

"Someone gave the order to attack. But where?" he asked.

The answer came when a B-40 rocket knocked a hole in the wall of the room where he sat with a headset on.

"Damn! We're being attacked!" he yelled over the air to anyone who wanted to listen.

His transmission was cut short as explosives were heard when mortar rounds pounded the tall radio and radar antennas at the installation. The tall towers started to crumble and fall in place.

The NPA had announced its arrival at the naval station with a loud hello.

The station's security was a contingent from Company C from the Marine Corps barracks. They were always armed and with loaded magazines. They counterattacked the NPA forces and started driving them back. The cost would be high, but they would secure their assigned post.

The two men cut through the wires at the Clark Air Base. When a hole was made, the rest of the NPA soldiers ran through. They ran as far as they could inside the huge military complex before they stopped, set up their mortars, and started firing at the aircraft on the runways.

Others fired shoulder-held B-40 rockets at barracks and hangars.

Clark AFB was caught flat footed when the mortars and B-40 rockets started coming in. Confusion reigned for a short while until sergeants and duty officers got some organization going to respond to the attack. Weapons and ammunition were issued. Men were ordered to report to their duty stations. People ran everywhere, flames from burning buildings and airplanes lighting the way.

The first to respond were the air force security teams. They, too, were always armed and ready to lock and load. Each team went to its designated area when the airfield came under attack. All their months and years of training for this moment was going to pay off. Air Base Security was also supported by the air force combat control teams stationed at the base. There was not a force large enough in the Philippines to take Clark away from them.

The attacking forces of the NPA were not able to reach any of the ships of the U.S. Navy at Subic Bay. The distance between the fence and the docks were too far and the security too strong. Company A, U.S. Marines, reacted with force. They quickly went to their assigned posts and started laying down a field of fire that could not be penetrated. A patrol from the 3rd Platoon, called the Jungle

Operations Branch, was on its way back to camp when the NPA hit the base. They mounted an attack on the rear of the Communist attackers. The NPA did not have a chance.

Sailors joined marines to defend their ships. A few fuel-storage tanks were hit by mortar and rocket fire and lit up the dark sky of the early morning.

Wallace Air Station of the U.S. Air Force was hit hard. Their small security force fought hard to keep the Communist forces from overrunning the base. Many of the planes were caught in the open, but most were saved because the airmen held the NPA forces far from the main storage and parking places of the aircraft.

The U.S. Air Force and U.S. Navy were able to get some of their aircraft aloft and out of harm's way. Most of the aircraft were not armed and ready to fight. They could only fly to the safety of the air and land on Filipino airfields that were not under attack when they ran low on fuel.

The attack was not doing much physical damage, but it put the Filipino and U.S. governments in an uproar.

Chuck woke Truck. "Colonel, the enemy has attacked Clark and Subic Bay that we know of. That's all the info I have now."

Truck got out of his bunk and put on his clothes. He strapped on his .45 pistol. He knew what he was going to do, and it meant war!

He walked across the compound to the command post of the camp commander. Colonel Peña was already in the CP.

"What've you got?" asked Truck.

Peña held up his hand, wanting Truck to hold. A radio man handed him a report. Peña looked it over quickly and then told Truck, "The NPA is attacking Subic Bay, Clark,

Cubi Point, and the Naval Communications Station in Zambales."

A soldier handed him another report. "Wallace Air Station over in La Union Province is under attack." Peña looked at Truck. "They are also attacking Philippine military bases, but their main efforts seem to be directed at U.S. bases."

Truck growled loudly.

Chuck entered the CP.

"Get the choppers and men ready," ordered Truck.

Chuck looked from him to Peña.

"Now, goddamn it!" Truck shot at him.

Chuck yelled, "Roger!" and left on the run. No one stood and looked Truck Grundy in that one good eye when there was fire blazing away in it.

"We do not yet have orders to attack the NPA with your Apache helicopters," Peña reminded Truck.

"Them bastards attacked the U.S. flag. They kill American men. That's enough for this old boy," Truck told him. There was no give in his voice. He asked Peña, "Will I have your peoples' support to hit Skull's fort?"

Peña hesitated only a moment before he said, "I will order it now."

"As soon as you get word from Bad Bear and Gutierrez, give me a call!" demanded Truck.

"It will be done," assured Peña.

Truck saluted and walked out of the CP. He had a job to do. He did not care much for politics or why the NPA thought they could get away with such a show of force. All this old trooper knew was that he had someone to fight and he had the equipment and men to do it with.

He saw the cluster of men waiting for him and walked to them.

Bo got out of his bunk and put on his flying clothes, pistol, and knife. He knew that if there was a fight in progress there would be only one reaction from Truck Grundy—get into it.

He had parked his O-1 near his barracks so it would be handy. His observer, a Filipino air force lieutenant, was to report directly to the plane if anything happened.

Bo reached the Bird Dog at the same moment as his observer. He called to him, "Alonzo, you ready to haul ass?"

"I'm with you, Colonel," the lieutenant returned. First Lieutenant Alonzo Santiago had no way of knowing that he was crawling into the backseat of an aircraft flown by one of the crazy "Ravens" from the Laotian war. He was going to be flying with the best and would have an experience to talk about for years to come.

The two men crawled into the aircraft and Bo fired up the engine. Bo checked his "bombs." They were mortar rounds, which he could drop out the window onto targets below. The Ravens had learned in Laos that a few mortar rounds could do a lot of damage and be the only support a unit got until fighter/bomber support arrived.

Bo kicked the engine over, waited for normal operating temperature to build up, kicked off the brakes, and taxied down the runway. He was airborne in a short distance. This man was now in his element. He believed it was his only element.

Truck walked to his Huey and reached for the hand mike of his radio. "Bo, I don't want no goddamned heroics."

Truck knew the Ravens well.

"I ain't no heroics, Truck. I's just a Bird Dog driver," Bo returned, laughing.

"Go do your job," Truck said unnecessarily. He turned back to his men. "Bo's our spotter. He'll try to go to the hottest spot. If he's got a target, he'll call and one of ya'll answer. Bo's an expert and knows what he's doing.

"We wait for Bad Bear before we head for the mountains and Skull's fort. We'll crank these things up and fly to any target of opportunity we find or we're called to fire upon."

The men ran toward their assigned Apaches. The Filipino ground crews had rolled the aircraft out from under the covered shed that had housed them from the sun and aerial view.

Push was running from helicopter to helicopter, checking each crew as they moved the Apaches into place. He yelled at each pilot as he walked past, "You don't take chances with this bird. I gotta put 'em back together when you screw 'em up. When you get low on fuel, get back here before you run outta juice. Don't come back with all your ordnance gone. You might run onto a problem coming back and you'll be defenseless."

The young warrant officer was venting his own spleen more than he was giving advice. When adrenaline flowed and you had nothing to hit, you screamed out loud to ease the pressure.

Truck flipped switches, cranked the engine on the Huey, and let the RPM run up to flight speed. He knew this bird was ready to fly. He had kept check on its maintenance until he found that the crew chief knew more about his job than he did. After that, he did his normal pilot check and let the Filipino flight crew do their thing.

His copilot was a Filipino Air Force captain named Armando Reyes. Two Filipino sergeants manned the door-guns. They were also members of the air force anti-insurgency force the Filipino government was developing.

They had never been on a large operation before and had been told that this one may be an all-out attack against Skull's fort. They were ready, for men think of glory and honor before they think of death and defeat.

Truck called over his radio to his men, "Keep that second radio channel open for navy radios. They communicate on strange freqs."

Willie watched as the rangers ran to stand by their assigned UH-1. They were all ready, their equipment tied down and their faces blackened. Their faces were even darker under the pale lights around the loading area. He was not bothered about going into combat with these men of a foreign army. He had spent much of his time working with men from other countries and had found good and bad among all of them. He would not rate this group until he found out how well they did in combat.

Hombros told Willie, "We can only stand by. We have no targets or mission for now. I'm not sure if they'll use us to counter the NPA or not."

Willie shrugged his shoulders. He was used to hurrying up and waiting. But he sure wanted to get into the fight.

The men lined up beside their assigned choppers and took off their gear to wait.

"It'd better be soon. The adrenaline is gonna be flowing out my ears," growled Willie.

Because Bad Bear was missing, only five Apaches were up. Chuck and Jumper flew together as Blue Team, and Red Dog and The Gooch flew as Green Team. Crackers was assigned to Red Team with Bad Bear, but in his absence, Truck had ordered him to fly with Red Dog and The Gooch.

The Communists had no air power. Truck had split the Apaches up into three two-chopper teams. They would fight together and support each other against ground attack.

Bo called over the air, with a lack of any real radio procedure, "C and C, I have ground firefight in sight. The location is at Naval Commo Station. Over."

Truck returned with, "Green Team, support Commo Station. Over."

"On the way. Out," Red Dog responded.

Truck keyed his radio and ordered, "Teams, I'm on my way to Cubi Point Station. Blue Team, support Wallace Air Station. Out."

Bo reached back for the night scope. He looked down at the people moving on the ground. They were the enemy. He gave a broad grin and pushed his stick down for a low pass over the enemy force.

He handed the scope back to his spotter. He called into the intercom, "Give me the word when we get over those bastards below."

"Roger, sir," the man told him and stuck the scope out the window for a better look. "Move over ten degrees to starboard."

Bo hit his right flap.

"Get ready . . . drop!" the spotter called.

Bo flipped out three mortar rounds.

Two rounds hit the right side of the plane and traveled up through the fuselage behind Red Dog and out the Plexiglas on the other side. The rounds missed both men and all vital lines of the aircraft.

"Whaaahoooo! Just like Laos and Nam!" yelled Bo.

He made another dive and dropped two more mortar rounds.

The Apaches came on station.

"Move over, little man, and let the big birds through," The Gooch called over the radio.

"Just do your job. I don't need no mouthing," Bo told him.

He flew off for other targets.

The Naval Communications Station was receiving support from U.S. Naval Air when Green Team arrived. The U.S. Navy took one look at the unmarked Apaches and called over their radios, "Who are you, Apache? Identify yourself immediately! Over."

Red Dog growled and pushed his radio button, "We are the guys that's gonna kick ass and take names of them NPA on the floor. Move over, jet jockies, and let us ground-support people do our thing. Out!"

A call was heard from U.S. Navy Control. "All Apaches in the air are friendlies. I repeat, all Apaches in the air are friendlies. Do you read me? Over!"

A number of "affirmatives" came over the air. One flier added, "Where the hell did Apaches come from?"

The Green Team did not hesitate to listen if everyone received the message. They attacked.

"Green Team, do your duty!" was Red Dog's only order.

The three Apaches picked out running members of the NPA and unloaded on them. Their TADS/PNVS system enabled them to see the figures in the early-morning darkness.

The fleeing people fired back with their automatic weapons, but the bullets hit the Apaches' armor and splattered into nothing. The rotor blades of the helicopters swatted small 7.62mm rifle ammunition as though they were no more than pesky mosquitoes.

Before long, the Apaches had what was left of an NPA attack on the run. Devastation of an air strike on the ground was magnificent to a soldier fighting an enemy trying to kill him.

All the Apaches had unleashed was their 30mm chain guns. They were saving their heavy load for larger targets.

The damage to the Communications Station was not extensive, except for the radar and radio antennas. Most of the large ones had been blown down, but many of the smaller ones were still up, allowing the navy to communicate. Several buildings were on fire, or already burned or blown to the ground. The sailors would have to spend a few days in tents until proper quarters were constructed.

A voice came over the air, "Who are those black devils?"

"A bunch of smart asses," a disgruntled voice came over the radio.

"I'm glad the boss thought of this second frequency so we could hear them navy boys," The Gooch called over his radio.

Crackers called back, "The boss is always way ahead of most people."

"You guys come back when ya got longer to stay," a navy flier called.

The Green Team flew their Apaches in zigzag maneuvers and flew off to rally on station until their control called.

By the time Blue Team got to Wallace Air Station, things were pretty much under control. The team identified itself as friendlies and finished mopping up the remainder of the NPA attack forces.

After their play at war, the team flew on station and waited order from control.

Truck could see the burning buildings before he arrived at Cubi Point Naval Air Station. Three Navy P-3C Orion antisubmarine aircraft were leaving the area when he arrived on station. With his Filipino markings, no one challenged him.

A voice called over the radio, "Do you have any more with you. Over."

"This is it. And it's all you need. Out!" Truck called back.

Truck put the nose of the UH-1 down toward the enemy and started searching for targets. He called over the intercom to the two sergeants, "Just keep the ammo flowing."

The crew did not take time to acknowledge.

Truck picked out the largest group of NPA and dived into the attack. The enemy fired back, their bullets singing past the attacking helicopter. Three rounds broke through the Plexiglas windows. Truck did not even duck. He kept his finger on the trigger and felt the vibration of the two guns dancing to their death song.

One of the crewmen in the back called out in pain.

Captain Reyes called over the intercom, "How bad is the wound?"

A voice called, "It's bad, Captain. He's dead."

Truck picked another target and dived to wreak havoc with the two roaring guns.

He made five attacking dives before he ran out of moving targets. Ground troops could finish up the rest of the enemy.

"Thanks for the assist," a voice called over the air.

Truck did not answer. He flew off, leaving the crew at the station to wonder who their flying warrior was. They would never learn his identity.

"Eagle Attack Team, return to base. I repeat, return to base," ordered Truck.

Two U.S. Air Force F-4Es out of Clark, the nose of their planes painted with tiger teeth and yellow slanted eyes, were flying overhead when they heard the call. One pilot called to the other, "Who or what in the hell is an Eagle Attack Team?"

"Another one of those mysteries of Asia," the other pilot returned.

15

No one reported the missing guard to Commander Skull. It was believed that the man, a heavy drinker and womanizer, left his post to go to the village in the valley.

Word had not yet reached the mountain of the NPA attacks. Skull had issued orders for strict radio silence long ago. He feared the government would use any radio transmission signals to home in on and find his location. All messages were transmitted by telephone and courier. The nearest telephone was in a safe house over an hour from the fort.

The NPA commander would not let Mano use any of the men from his mountain security. He insisted that his headquarters must be secured for the benefit of the movement.

When word did reach the fort about the attacks, Skull was in his favorite spot in the bunker eating breakfast. He liked to sit and look over the valley from his vantage point high in the mountains.

He read the report he received. It appeared the attacks were not going well. But he did not expect such small forces to overrun each target. His hope was that the people would come to the side of his cause, and that was to get rid of the American military bases. He would have to wait for his spies' reports to come in to see how well his propagandists and fifth columnists did their job.

Other reports came in that there were no soldiers in the area or any aircraft in the air flying over the mountains. That meant that the government still had no idea where his headquarters was located. His haven was safe from the outside, but even if it was not, he had antiaircraft weapons to stop any air attack against him. He also had a strong ground reserve that would come to his assistance if needed.

Reports came in from his spies during the day, and they were not good. How could the people be in favor of a government that allowed a foreign country to remain upon its sovereign soil?

"I do not understand these people! Are they so dense? Are they all uneducated peons that they don't know what is going on in their own country? How can they not rise up and throw the foul Americans out of our country?"

Skull was beside himself. He threw his hands up into the air and walked in circles inside the bunker.

A man came to the door. He stopped and waited.

"Yes! What do you want?" Skull shouted.

"People are marching in the streets in Manila and Quezon City—" the man started but was cut off.

"Well it's about time!" retorted Skull.

"But pardon, sir, if you please. They march to protest the kidnapping of the Ybarra children," the man told his angry commander.

"What? What did you say?" Skull exploded.

"Serna, he captured Ybarra and Ybarra's three schoolchildren," the man said after a gulp. He stood, ready to duck or run. He knew he may have to do both.

"You are here to tell me he kidnapped children? That imbecile kidnapped children?" he shouted. No one had seen Skull so angry and out of control. He was a very cruel man even in the best circumstances. Everyone would have to be on watch.

The man stood, flinching. Things must be going badly, indeed.

"Give me the report," barked Skull, holding out his hand for the written report. He scanned it over, a dark look coming over his face.

Skull stopped his pacing and stood a moment. He finally went to his chair and slumped into it. "My God, he took children by force. Doesn't the ass know that children are sacred to our people? What have I got following me, complete *estupidos*? God! Do I have to command and do everything?"

The messenger saluted and backed quickly out of the door.

Skull's little bed partner walked over behind his master and started rubbing his neck and shoulders.

"Get out! Get out, you filthy-mouthed *varon puta*! Get off this mountain and don't ever come back!" shouted Skull.

The man beat a hasty retreat.

A woman who was on her way with the midmorning coffee turned on her heels and went back to the kitchen. She would return at a later time.

Two junior commanders who had been standing by quietly left the room. They hoped they could leave before they were seen.

Skull sat, a dark shadow cast over his face and his eyes blazing in anger. He had spent months planning for an uprising and planning for a way to drive the Americans out of the country and the Philippine government out of office. His most ambitious plan was to drive a wedge between the Filipino and American governments. Now he was being stopped by an idiot. The report said two of Ybarra's children were girls. He always knew that Serna's penis was larger than his brain.

Skull was near crying in frustrated anger.

But he still had his fort.

Truck was sitting in the CP when the call came in that the patrol requested a pickup. He told Peña that he was going along for the ride.

He got in the chopper and rode in the backseat with the crew chief and door gunner. He wanted that report first-hand, then he would do some planning on his way back to camp.

The pilot circled the pickup point once and then sat the UH-1 down in the small clearing. Bad Bear and the three Filipinos ran out of the tree line and jumped into the helicopter.

After greeting each other, Truck handed Bad Bear a helmet with an intercom system.

"What ya got, Bear?" asked Truck.

"I saw one each, a ZPU-4 and an M1939 antiaircraft weapon," replied Bad Bear. "Each of 'em was in a separate hooch. Ya count the number of hooches, we might figure out how many antiaircraft weapons. We just won't know the size until we get there and they start shooting."

"I like little surprises," said Truck dryly. "How about missiles?"

"Didn't see any," replied Bad Bear. "I reckon all they got, *pah-bee*, are shoulder-held missiles."

"If fired right, they'll knock an Apache out of the air,"

insisted Truck. "And they can damned sure bring pee on UH-1s and fixed-wings."

"You got enough info to start planning," Bad Bear told him. There was no doubt to the Kiowa that Truck's mind was already working up a plan. All he would have to do was talk it over with Peña and the others, put it onto paper in an operation order, then prosecute it. He sat back and relaxed. He had done his job, and he had been up all night.

Gutierrez was looking relaxed and droopy eyed. The two sergeants had already gone to sleep.

Bad Bear smiled. Now, that's the way to fight a war. Let somebody else worry about the big stuff.

"Bear, which one of these hooches was the M1939 in?" asked Truck.

Bad Bear looked at the aerial photo and pointed to one of the hooches. He looked at Gutierrez and asked, "You agree, Lieutenant?"

"That is the way I call it," responded Gutierrez.

"We see six huts that we believe contain antiaircraft guns," said Peña. "The one big problem we have is no knowledge of the sizes of the weapons in the other huts."

"There's no doubt about the M1939 knocking hell out of an Apache if it cuts loose on one," Truck told the men. "That thing's only got one barrel, but it's a 37mm tube. That's an old weapon, built to fire at old World War Two fighters and bombers. So that means it's hell on helicopters. I know it drove off a lot of Hueys in Southeast Asia."

"If we'd a had more time to plan the patrol and run it, we coulda found out what was in each of them huts," said Bad Bear.

"No, Bear, you men did good with the time you had. If you'd done more moving around the fort, you might have been spotted. Let's eliminate as much screw-up as we can.

We do that by not taking fate by the nose and kicking it in the ass," replied Truck. He accepted the coffee handed him. He took a drink. It was good and strong. These rangers believed in "airborne coffee."

Truck continued, "We know we wanna hit that M1939 first. We'll just have to wait for the roofs to be thrown back and the other guns to start banging away before we can learn the size of the others. We'll just have to be smart enough to attack that one and keep our choppers out of harm's way until we find out where all the big guns are."

"We can't attack all six at once?" asked Captain Castello.

"No. Those guns are arranged so we can't get to all of them at once. We'll just have to take out one while supported by the other Apaches and go like hell," replied Peña. "The man who set these guns up knew his business."

"Besides, we're gonna have to use some of the Apaches to support the ground attack. We'll have to use UH-1 gunships to support the ground units neutralizing the reserves," said Truck. He pointed to the map at the different locations where reserves were believed to be kept. "We have planned, Colonel Romeros and me, to use Hombros and his men to attack the main fort and see if they can locate Skull. We will use the other rangers and air force commandos to block the reserves."

"Good idea," commented Chuck, still studying the map and photos.

"It seems from the aerial photos we have of the other forts that they don't have antiaircraft guns in place. If they have any aircraft weapons at all, it will be shoulder-fired SAMs. So we'll have to watch out for them," Truck informed them.

"We must plan our operation," reminded Peña.

The rest of the men left the commanders and staff to plan the operation order.

Truck and Peña got with Major Cavazos, the camp's S-3, and discussed the operations plan. After the staff finished the plan and it met with the approval of Peña, a briefing was called. The pilots, copilots, ranger leaders, and air commando leaders were called to the operations building. The assistant S-3 passed out the operations order and strip maps. The staff gave their part of the operations order, reporting on known enemy locations, on the weather, communications, logistics, personnel, and the attack plan. It was a good briefing and plan. These men had read the book, as Truck was wont to say. The coordinated attack on the NPA was to begin at o-four-hundred hours.

After the briefing and questions and answers, the formal meeting broke up. Men remained behind to talk about their missions and look over the large maps and aerial photos.

Truck turned to Bo and said, "Bo, keep a lookout for radar. When we find one, maybe between the two of us we can get a fix on the thing."

"Roger. If I connect with one, I'll call you. I'll fly straight into it, that way the line'll stay straight. Then the guys with the maps can get a fix where our two lines meet," replied Bo.

"Radars may be with the guns, but they may be set back or are mobile for their protection," Truck informed him. "But if they're turned on, we'll be able to find 'em."

"Either way they're sitting, they'll be effective. Even if they don't have experienced radar operators and gunners, they have enough experienced mathematicians that can figure the angles and adjust the gunfire," explained Peña. He was commenting on the large amount of college students and higher-educated people that were in the NPA.

"Them guys are just educated, they ain't smart," growled Bo.

"And you watch flying straight into those radar beams. It could get you killed," Truck told Bo.

"Right, Dad," growled Bo, just as though he had never done it before.

The men started breaking up and going to their units to get their gear and equipment ready for combat.

Bad Bear gave a thumbs-up as he left the building.

16

The Americans sat in the small living area of their quarters. Each man was busy with his own equipment, getting ready to kill or be killed. This was a fact they never thought much about. They just did their duty as soldiers and let the rest of life take care of itself.

"Bad Bear, I told you where I got the name Jackson, so where'd you get your name?" asked Push.

"That's my family name. Sate-Zalebay means 'Bad Bear' in Kiowa," he explained. "Sate is bear. A warrior who is given the name of Bear is indeed a great warrior of his people. The name Bad is even a greater warrior. A good name to have. One of the most famous with the name Sate is one of my ancestors, Sate-Tanta, 'White Bear.' You whites, you yellows, and you blacks call him Satanta in your history."

"If your family is Bad Bear, your people must have taken it from a great warrior in the family," said Crackers.

"So we're told," admitted Bad Bear. "My grandfather

still tells tales the old men told him when he was a little boy. They still sing songs at powwows around Carnegie, Oklahoma. That's where the U.S. government put the Texas Plains Indians called the Kiowa, my people. Each of the old warrior families have their own songs. When it's played, the whole family dances. When the song of the great Sate-Tanta is played, it is like a sacred song to the Kiowa people. He is still greatly honored.

"The old people tell us the bear is sacred to the Kiowa. He is a great warrior and great medicine. My people will not kill a bear. That is for others to do. They must have the right medicine, or it will be bad for them."

"Were you raised on a reservation?" asked Push.

"No. There is only one reservation in Oklahoma. That's the Osage Indians up north. There have been no other reservations in Oklahoma since 1907, when it became a state," replied Bad Bear. "When Indian Territory became a state, they took all the land away from the Indians and gave it to the White man. They gave each head of an Indian family one hundred sixty acres for all his people and said, 'Now, go dig and plant corn and be happy.' My grandfather told me they said be happy because they didn't kill all of us. But you try to get enough corn to grow in Oklahoma, where I live, and all of your people will starve.

"The white men waited until we all got real hungry, then they came and leased Indian land to run cattle. That is what we were supposed to live on. It is hard sometimes to be an Indian."

"Hell, it's hard to be anybody sometimes," put in Crackers.

"Don't kill bears? They're sacred? That's a crock of shit. Ain't nothing sacred," laughed The Gooch.

"The bear is sacred to a Kiowa. We can't kill it, or we will have big trouble," said Bad Bear. He took a drink of

Kool-Aid. Beer was forbidden at a time like this. "I will not kill it. That's all I can say about it."

"You really believe all that stuff?" asked The Gooch, the street kid from the city.

"Yep. I don't reason why or ask questions about it. It's been too long with my people. Why, or how, should someone like me ask or question the validity of such things?" returned Bad Bear.

"Asking questions and doubting is what put the white man on top of the heap," said The Gooch in a disgusted voice. No one told The Gooch what to think.

"What heap?" asked Bad Bear. "The drug heap? The woman-beating and child-molesting heap? The incest heap? The destruction-of-Mother-Earth-and-all-of-her-children, the-waters-and-the-plants-and-animals heap?"

"Well, hell, there's some good points in our heap," said The Gooch. He was getting a little angry at the way the conversation was going.

"Yeah, when you brought the red man whiskey and measles, you made yourself a good heap. A great people puts themselves on top of heaps that way," Bad Bear said with a growl. He got up and said, "I ain't gonna talk about it no more."

There was a finality in his voice that was noticed by all except The Gooch.

"Well, by God, I ain't finished," The Gooch stated, and got up to head Bad Bear off.

Bad Bear ignored him and went out the door.

"Gooch, drop it," ordered Truck.

"Like hell," The Gooch shot back.

"It ain't a request," said Truck. "Not only because I like Bear and we're brothers, but because he'll kill you. I don't want that. You guys wanna beat up on somebody, wait 'til o-four-hundred hours. Then it's open season on who ya can get in your sights."

"I'll buy that," said Crackers.

"Anytime and any day," added Jumper.

Push nodded his head.

The Gooch grumbled and kicked things beside his bunk, but otherwise he remained silent.

Red Dog was unconcerned about the situation. There could have been a killing and he would have shrugged it off.

Chuck gave a sigh of relief when Truck had stepped in and stopped the talk between the men. He knew there were times when men's tempers flared while they were getting ready for the kill. It seemed to be even stronger among some professional soldiers who had been in battle many times. They were geared up for the kill long before they got into battle and would fight at the drop of the well-known hat. Yet they would risk their own life to save their fellow soldier when the enemy tried to take it.

The rest of the evening was spent quietly.

Colonel Rufus Holguin met with Brigadier General Dan Olive on Smoke Bomb Hill.

Dan asked, "What've you heard from our boy?"

"Nothing, Dan. He's got the ball and he'll run with it," Rufus assured him. "And he'll do it right."

"Goddamn! The old man's jumping straight up and down," stated Dan. Then he grinned. "So are those guys in Washington. No one knows what the hell's going on in the Philippines."

"Truck and the team went out to their secret launch site after I was in the Philippines the last time. If anything is going down, you can bet your bottom dollar Truck and crew are in the middle of it," said Rufus. "But, damn, Dan, that's what we sent them there for."

"I know, I know. The old A-team leader in me. I think I gotta be in on everything or things are going to get screwed up," explained Dan. "One of the worst things about being a general is you sit in an office and don't know what the hell's going on until it's finished or it gets screwed up."

"There has been no news reports of Apaches in the air when the Communist forces hit our bases," said Rufus. "But you can bet that they were somewhere, doing something. I know Truck. When they attacked the flag, they attacked him personally."

"When they attacked the flag and started killing Americans, they attacked all of us personally," growled Dan. "If the press hears about Apaches flying around with Americans in them, they'll have a field day. They won't give a damn about Resolution 445 or any other resolution. All they'll scream is that American boys are getting killed. Hell! If you don't use your military, you might as well disband the damned thing."

The general walked out to the outer office and checked the coffee maker. It had done its duty and he poured himself and Rufus a cup and went back into his office. He handed Rufus a cup.

"We knew that coming in," stated Rufus.

"I know," admitted Dan.

"The Apaches have Filipino air force officers in each one of them," Rufus reminded him. "Remember, Truck demanded that? He said the Filipinos would have accountability if one of them went down with an American in it. The Americans were merely contract pilots teaching the Filipinos how to fly those things."

Dan looked at Rufus over his coffee cup. He said around the cup, "This is sad, Rufus. Goddamn sad. Don't become a general. You start thinking like a politician—worrying more about making that second star than what's right for your troops. Hell, when I was a colonel, I'd tell the generals how it oughta be done, then push for getting it done right, the military way, by God. That's the only right way I know of."

Rufus grinned. "That's the reason you got me around, Dan. To keep you straight. Why in the hell do you think they kept you around when you was a colonel?"

Dan returned the grin.

The two men sat and finished their coffee.

"Well, there's one thing that's certain. Them poor bastards has got one of the best men I know against them," Dan said happily. "I'd say they ain't got a snowball's chance in Florida."

Rufus left the general's office feeling better himself. It was now up to Truck and his people. And the general was right. The higher your rank, the less control you seemed to have. It was nothing like being in the thick of things. He missed it—the feeling of being really alive and accomplishing something. He also missed the troops.

General Ruiz sat in his office, waiting for Colonel Ramos. No one had gotten any sleep since the early-morning attack by the NPA. It would be a longer time before anyone would get any sleep or rest before this was over with. Communist attacks and abductions had put the entire country in an upheaval.

He took another drink of the strong coffee.

He was so disgusted with his people. The Philippines had a chance to be a true democratic country and what do these stupid idiots do? he asked himself for the millionth time. Simple-minded army officers make coup after coup against an elected administration. The Communists used the uncertainty to foster mistrust and to attack the establishment. They were trying to get the Americans kicked out of the

Philippines, the one true friend the country had. The Moros were still trying, after all these many years, to gain control of their own destiny and kick out a liberal government that lets them have religious freedom.

His thoughts were interrupted by his aide announcing Ramos.

"Ah, Ramos, what news have you?" asked Ruiz.

"Well, General, things may be different in our country in the morning. Peña and the Americans are going to attack Skull's fort at zero-four-hundred hours. With those great helicopters and experienced American soldiers flying them, I think Skull's rule will come to an end before noon tomorrow," said Ramos with a smile.

"So soon? You think they can win the battle so soon?" asked the general. Then he said, "You have great faith in those American helicopters."

"Yes, I do. It would be next to impossible for our forces to successfully attack Skull's fort with all the mortars, artillery and dug-in emplacements he has. Our air support would be little or nothing with all the antiaircraft weapons he has on that mountain," Ramos reminded him. "With those flying tanks, we have a chance to put troops on that mountain and bring Skull's body out."

"Are you sure they'll bring his body out?" asked Ruiz.

"Hombros himself said he didn't want another prisoner to escape and be the cause of more of our people's death," was Ramos's short answer.

"Good."

"And for assurances on how well the Americans are doing with our people, I can only say what Peña told me. He said these Americans were some of the most professional, experienced soldiers he has had the pleasure to serve with," Ramos informed him. "These men are experts at working with foreign nationals. They have fought with men from many different armies. They treat our people as their own."

"That is good," was the general's only reply. But inside he was grateful that such men had been sent to work with his people. "This group of Americans are low key and keep their business from the public as much as possible. That means they will let our people have much of, if not all, the credit. That is good. We won't have our political enemies and detractors saying that we again had to go to the Americans to help us with our own problems."

"I told you these were good people," bragged Ramos.

"Colonel, we both have jobs to do. I suggest we do them."

Ramos stood, saluted, and left the room.

Things were looking up. Now if they could only locate where Ybarra and his children were being held. And if the anti-insurgency forces were going to attack early in the morning, he may as well stay up and not go home, he thought.

He smiled to himself. Yes, it was going to be a long night.

He took another drink of coffee that had gone lukewarm and shuddered at its bitterness.

17

The Apaches were rolled out of the covered stands on their own wheels. Wheels had replaced the skids used by the Huey and Cobra. The Apaches had two front wheels and a rear wheel like the old fixed-winged tail draggers.

Truck had assigned the Blue Team, with Chuck and Jumper, to take out the known position of the Soviet-built M1939 antiaircraft gun. The Green Team, with Red Dog and The Gooch, was to fly support for Blue Team and try to locate large-caliber weapon positions. It would be a dangerous game of search and destroy, but that was part of the job.

The Red Team, with Bad Bear and Crackers, was to support the ranger assault team, led by Hombros, which was going to attack the fort from the rear by landing on the top of the mountain. Truck and Peña believed the ground attack would have a better chance from this direction because from their analysis of the aerial photos it appeared that there were less defensive weapons pointed that way.

Skull must have made much of his defense on the presumption that men could not land in the thick forest of the mountaintop and that he had enough defensive weapons to stop any frontal or flank attack.

Bad Bear was a combat infantry sergeant before he got his warrant officer's commission to fly helicopters. He understood and appreciated close air support. There was not a better man to support the ground attack team.

Chuck's Apache had been armed with the three Hellfire missiles. Red Dog was armed with the other three missiles. The warheads of the rockets would eliminate any gun located on the mountain. The rest of their load was made up of 70mm rockets with delayed fuses for destroying bunkers.

The rest of the choppers were also armed with 70mm rockets with delayed fuses. They would depend upon their chain guns for antipersonnel weapons.

Truck would fly as control for the attack on Skull's main fort. He would engage targets of opportunity.

Peña would fly as control for the attack on the reserves and attacks upon the other forts in the area. The air force commandos would fly support and the remaining ranger and the marine force would attack the reserves to keep them pinned down.

The equipment and men were ready. The Filipino high command at Fort Bonifacio had provided extra helicopter support for the operation. The troops would be transported to the attack in a number of shuttles. There were only forty-five UH-1 helicopters in the entire Philippine air force, so helicopters were limited.

The Philippine army would send more troops by land convoy to reach the area by two hours after daylight.

Peña and Truck checked their watches. It was time to start getting "saddled up."

The men flying the Apaches and Philippine air commando gunships were the first to load up. They were the first attack wave. If they failed, the mission would fail.

Heavy mortars and artillery would be useless during the attack because of the terrain and forest. The rangers would take their small 60mm mortars for support. The ground forces would also have the helicopters on call for ground support.

The Apache crews walked to their helicopters in groups. Each flight team walked as one, four men in each team.

Bad Bear was flying, but he had marked his face with black war paint as if he were in the main ground attack. A warrior was a warrior no matter what his place on the battlefield was.

The Gooch saw Bad Bear in the pale light and gave him a thumbs-up.

Bad Bear returned the signal.

These two men had been at each other's throats in anger a short while before, but now they were on their way to fight a common enemy. All animosity for each other had left and would now be directed toward the dug-in Communists.

The men got into their aircraft and put on their safety harnesses. They placed their helmets on, slipping their target acquisition and designation sight/pilot's night vision sensor over one eye. In the pale instrument lights, the TADS/PNVS device over one eye made the crews looks like modern-day pirates. When switches were flipped on for a functional check, the chain gun turned in the direction the gunner was looking. The swiveling gun looked like a huge beak or a stinger on a live metal monster.

Truck had found one main vulnerability with the Apache, and that was the exposed swiveling action of the M230 30mm Hughes Chain Gun. The weapon was an outstanding piece of equipment, functioned properly, fired up to 750 rounds per minute, and was death on armored vehicles as well as ground personnel. But an unlucky hit on the unprotected gun from a small-arms round or a flying piece of shrapnel would put it out of action. He would like to have some armor around that swivel action.

The signal was given, and off the Apaches flew in team formation. The ground team attacking the reserves would have farther to fly and took off shortly after the Apaches. They had to be in place when the Apaches started their attack.

Team Red and the attacking force of rangers waited to give the attacking Apaches time to start hitting the target before the ground troops would be committed. Team Red would depart on a set time schedule unless notified otherwise.

Chuck led the two teams out. He flew over the spot in the camp where he had shot an azimuth with his compass, got the correct reading on his instruments, and flew northeast. The other three Apaches flew as his wing men. It was a habit he had picked up in the old days, before all the new equipment that could set a correct course from anyplace on earth—or maybe in the universe.

Captain Castello flew the front seat in Chuck's helicopter. Castello had quickly learned the complicated system of the Apache. He had not learned it to perfection, but well enough to do his job with a few questions and answers between the two men on the intercom. Chuck knew he was going to work out. This was not the Filipino captain's first time to face live rounds coming at him. He had been an air force commando from the first and had been engaged in every coup attempt and most of the actions against the NPA and Moros.

Chuck was an old hand at this. He had passed the rank in service of being an individual pilot for a helicopter attack in the regular navy. But here being with this group, he had a chance to go out and fight with front-line troops before he left the navy. He was glad he had taken the assignment and had gotten out of the Pentagon desk job. He always hated such assignments.

He knew this mission was going to take all the skills he had as a pilot of an attack helicopter. He was leading a flight of choppers into a target that was known to have antiaircraft weapons that could knock out an Apache. There were also missiles that were unaccounted for, and that made him nervous. Not the type of nervousness that made him want to turn back from the mission. But the type that made for caution and kept people alive. Chuck was again leading men into a life-and-death situation. The job was not made for the weak of heart.

The attacking force was to keep radio silence until they were committed or they were in the actual attack. Skull's camp would have radios listening to all the known radio frequencies the military used.

Bad Bear checked his watch and lifted off. He flew in the lead of the ground attack force. He loved to fly, but he wished he was in one of the Hueys going in with Willie and the rangers. Eyeball-to-eyeball contact with the enemy was the way for a warrior to go to combat. But he had learned over the years that there were many positions on the battlefield for a warrior in this modern war. As a pilot and a member of this group, he was able to be in all the positions of a warrior, both on the ground and in the air. He was glad that he and Truck had become close friends years ago when he was a young sergeant and Truck was an old captain. He knew from the first that Truck was part of his

destiny. Destiny played a big part in the lives of most
American Indians. He was no different from any other
Kiowa.

He could see the back of the helmet of the young Filipino
air force pilot in front of him. The man had been working
out well and was a fast learner. Bad Bear hoped the man
would stand strong and do his job when bullets started
flying his way. He was a good judge of men and felt he had
a winner sitting in the front seat.

In his mind he could see that big black guy Willie
Falloure sitting on the web seat of the UH-1, grinning at the
men around him. Willie liked combat nearly as much as he
and Truck did. Willie was a warrior, just as he and Truck
were. Willie was a good man.

Willie looked down at the rugged terrain below, seeing its
dark outline against the sky. These mountains were worse
than anything he had seen in Vietnam. They were like those
he had fought in and across with the Meo tribesmen in Laos.
Now, there were some mountains. These looked just as bad,
if not worse in places. He knew there would be no
twenty-mile days in the bush down there—not even with
trails.

There was no more apprehension in Willie than there was
in Truck and Bad Bear, or the other guys. This was his
profession, this being at war with hot lead flying and the
adrenaline pumping strong. This was his life. This made life
worth living. If he had not loved his profession and lived in
fear of war, he would have changed to a civilian suit and a
nine-to-five job a long time ago.

He grinned at the young troops sitting on the floor of the
chopper. They would have a story to tell their grandchildren. Of course, not all would live through this attack to tell
it.

• • •

Truck saw the small O-1 Bird Dog flying lazily around the area as if he were on a sightseeing tour. But he knew Bo Peep Day was only waiting for the action to start. Then he would climb just high enough over the battle action to give good reports on enemy and gun locations. When Bo Peep gave a report on a target, it would always be an accurate one. He hoped the Filipino captain observer would be as ready when the shit started flying as he was back in camp. Flying with Bo could be a heart stopper.

To his right front flew the attack Apaches. They were nap-flying close to the rugged terrain to keep out of radar view. The instruments in the Apache made this type of flying possible at night, in fog or clouds.

He watched them turning more to the east to get into position to attack Skull's fort. Chuck would lead his attack force in from the left flank of the enemy.

Truck felt the surge of adrenaline at the thought of the attack. He was ready for the action to start. Too long between fights made a man rusty. He liked to keep his edges honed to a razor sharpness.

He looked over at his copilot, Captain Armando Reyes. Truck called over the intercom, "I think we're getting close to attack time."

Reyes took a quick look at his watch and said with a grin, "It is now three minutes until we attack."

Truck would have to relay his messages to the ground forces through a radio man in the back of the helicopter, but he had direct radio contact with the men in the air.

The Eagle Attack Team was about to make their venture into combat as an organization for the first time.

18

The Apache rose up above the crest of the ridge to get a good sight picture on the hut with the M1939 antiaircraft weapon. The flying machine seemed to appear from no-where out of the depths of the thick fog. The mist of the fog made the targets hard to see under normal conditions, but with the Apache's forward-looking infrared, or FLIR, system, the crew could fly through fog and clouds and sight in on any target. With this system, all the pilots had to do was follow the images on the screen located on the panels in front of them.

They broke through the heaviest part of the fog just as they came on station.

Chuck held the Apache steady while Castello zeroed in on the hut in front of them.

Jumper pulled his helicopter up to the left of Chuck, ready to open fire on any enemy weapon and to give support to his teammates.

Castello sighted in on the target. He could not see it as

plainly through the TADS/PNVS as he could in normal daylight, but he could see the hut well enough to hit it with a missile. He actually did not have to see the target. As long as the infrared beam could pick out the target, that was all that was needed. He quickly sighted, read off the numbers from the instruments on the side of the sighting device, and fired off a Hellfire missile. The missile flew straight and true, following the gunner's initial laser-beam sighting to the target. Once the little controller in the Hellfire was set on a target, no evasive maneuver could dodge its flight. A target sitting still was no challenge at all.

The hut disappeared in the early-morning darkness in a fire ball of flying splinters and metal as the weapon and hut disintegrated. The fireball was bright in the night-seeing device the pilots and gunners wore.

All of this had only taken a few short seconds.

Chuck flew in search of other targets. He knew that the enemy would swing into action before long.

Jumper took action on the next known target, the hut housing the ZPU-4 four-barreled antiaircraft gun. He told the gunner, "Hit that thing with a few chain-gun rounds. That oughta shake 'em up."

Jumper had no sooner finished speaking than the gunner touched off the 30-millimeter chain gun. Red flame followed the rounds to the target. A few bursts later and hut and gun inside were completely destroyed.

After the initial attack, the Apache pilots started systematically firing on all the huts and bunkers.

The NPA recovered from the surprise attack and started returning fire. Roofs were thrown back on the huts and sides dropped to allow the antiaircraft weapons to open up at the attacking helicopters. Confusion reigned within the NPA fort, for these men had never been under attack before.

There were no actual contingency plans nor had there been exercises to prepare for the defense of the fort.

Skull jumped out of his bed and stood still in amazed horror. Who would make such a bold move to attack his fort? He stayed in place naked and confused for a moment. He grabbed his pants and shoes and jumped into the tunnel that led to his command bunker. He stumbled along, trying to put his pants on as he ran through the tunnel. He left a frightened girl in his bed. She vanished in the blast of chain-gun fire that dismantled the hut and all within it.

Commander Skull had gotten his wish—that was for someone to attack his reinforced fort. He grinned, knowing his antiaircraft weapons would knock anything out of the air the Philippine military had. He waited impatiently to hear the big guns start firing or the *whoosh* of a missile.

Instead, he heard the boom of a missile hitting one of his defensive positions.

"Fire!" he screamed. "Shoot them down!"

Skull was screaming orders as he ran into the CP bunker. He grabbed the handset of the radio and started shouting orders.

A Hellfire missile shook the command bunker to its foundations. Its shape-charge warhead was as effective on the bunker as it was on an armored tank. Then a steady rain of 70mm rockets started chipping away at the top and walls of his broken refuge. He had to run for his life, seeking shelter in other parts of his network of tunnels and bunkers. From the outset of the attack, he was never in control of his forces defending his fort.

A staccato of small-arms rounds hit Red Dog's helicopter. His teeth were bared by a grin as he pointed the Apache in the direction the fire was coming from. The gunner sighted in on the target and pushed the button, unleashing two rockets on the machine-gun emplacement, and followed with a burst of 30mm chain-gun fire. The machine-gun bunker was demolished.

He could see men and weapons disintegrate in the glow of the TADS/PNVS.

His grin grew larger as he started slowly scanning the mountainside for new targets. Whenever he and his copilot/gunner saw a bunker complex, lethal fire spewed from all the weapons of the Apache. He was going to do his best to clear as many defensive positions as he could before Willie and the ground attack force arrived. Those guys had nothing between them and the enemy harder than the buttons on their fatigue jackets.

The Apaches had a system in their computers that talked to the other Apaches around it, keeping the others from firing on the same targets. Such a system was needed when fighting in such close quarters as this.

Red Dog was getting low on ammo. He called off station for he had to go home and reload. The Gooch fell in behind him.

Push, Sarhento Garcia, and their crew were going to be very busy the next few hours. But who would not be?

In a few minutes both of the Green Team's Apaches were serviced and they flew back to their attack positions. The service vehicle had to be reloaded for the next team that would come in for a refill.

The Gooch got back in time to meet an antiaircraft weapon. A burst of fire from a ZPU-4 splattered against the armor of The Gooch's helicopter. It came from his left. He swung the chopper around, pointing it in the direction the fire was coming from. Gooch held the chopper steady, moving slowly in a sideways crawl until he and the gunner spotted the gun emplacement.

A shoulder-held SAM missile was fired from directly

below him. The round whizzed past the chopper. He was so low to the ground that the missile flew on its own, not homing in on the exhaust from his engines.

The Gooch pitched the rotors and started backing up, trying to outmaneuver the gunner of the shoulder-fired missile. But he was still so low to the ground that the second round was also unaffected by the chopper's "Black Hole" infrared suppressor system. The missile had time to arm itself in the short flight and it hit the nose of the helicopter. The explosion took off the front part of the Apache and part of the rotor. The aircraft fell like a kid's broken toy.

The chopper crashed into the side of the mountain, not exploding on contact. A fire started burning inside the engine compartment.

"Goddamn!" moaned a stunned Gooch. He tried to move his legs to support himself in his awkward position. He could not feel either leg. He tried to move his right arm, but it was caught in a mangle of metal and heavy bulletproof Plexiglas. He tried to reach his knife on his webbing but could not reach it. His arm was so mangled, it barely moved. Truck had insisted that all the pilots have a large-bladed knife fixed to their webbing just in case they were caught in a wreckage if shot down. If the damned thing started burning, they could use the knife to cut a leg or arm off to free themselves.

Small-arms rounds started marching down the mountainside toward the downed helicopter. Men came out of their bunkers to capture or finish off the men.

The Gooch raised his head enough so that he could see the men. He knew that one of the many things he did not want was to be captured.

"I smell smoke," came through broken lips. Another thing he could do without was being burned alive.

His mind strained to move his arm. Nothing. He used his

fingers to creep up to the button that would set off the explosives to destroy the helicopter. His fingers found the safety guard. He fumbled until he got it worked off. The enemy soldiers were getting closer.

"You guys ain't gonna get this little street boy. I'm gonna get on my street chopper and ride on outta here," grumbled The Gooch.

He looked up at the back of the helmet of his Filipino copilot. "Ya did a good job, little man. But this here street biker ain't gonna let them hoods get their hands on me. Not while I'm alive."

He waited for the men to get closer. He was not going alone. He pushed the switch forward. The explosion shook the mountainside, the blast cutting down huge trees and men as well. There was not enough left to identify the two pilots of the AH-64 Apache.

"Chopper down. The Gooch has gone in," Red Dog reported over the air.

Red Dog saw the NPA soldiers moving out to the downed helicopter. He dived down, raking the enemy with the chain gun. The trees started blocking his line of fire. He used the gun to cut down trees to clear a path to fire on targets. He had completely taken over control of the guns from the copilot.

He next saw the explosion when The Gooch detonated the explosives wired to the craft and pieces of the downed Apache hit the bottom of his helicopter.

"Damn!" Red Dog paused, and then announced over the air, "The Gooch has bought the farm."

The old air force pilot turned his helicopter back toward the main defenses of the NPA. "I'm gonna get ya, ya dirty bastards. Ya killed one of my boys, one of my friends, and I'm gonna get ya."

His next report was, "I'm going back to rearm."

There was now a hole in their attack line. Chuck and Jumper had to hold the line until Red Dog returned and they could go rearm and have their Apaches serviced.

Two rounds from an M1939 caught Chuck's helicopter, penetrating the engine compartment and knocking out the starboard engine completely. The other engine started to stutter and cough in its mighty whirring sound.

"We're going in," Chuck called over the air. He tried to bring the helicopter into an auto-gyro mode, but he was too low for it to take effect. The heavy helicopter crashed through the trees to the ground with a heavy impact.

"Hang on, Chuck, I'll cover you," Truck called into the mike attached to his helmet.

He dived down to the smoking Apache. He saw that Chuck's aircraft was shielded from direct fire from the NPA by a ridge. He dropped down lower to get out of the sights of the M1939 gun and hovered over the crash in case they sent out foot elements to try and capture Chuck and Castello.

Chuck was stunned by the crash. He opened his eyes to see that his chopper was not on fire. Unusual as hell, went through his mind. And no explosion. I must be about out of rockets.

His right leg hurt. It was pinned in the wreckage and he could not move it. He moved his toes in his left boot. They moved! So did his hands and fingers. No back damage, he thought happily.

"Chuck. Do you read me? Over," called Truck.

"I read you. We ain't going nowhere," Chuck told him. Then he tapped Castello on the helmet. "You alive?"

There was no response.

"Chuck. Stay put. Medics and Medevac are on the way," Truck called to him. "Wait. Help is on its way."

We're not going anywhere. The words did not come.

Chuck knew that his leg was mangled beyond repair. I won't be able to fly anymore. I'll be kicked out of the navy! flashed through his mind.

He had no way of knowing whether Castello was alive or not.

I must wait. I must wait for the Jolly Green Giant. The Jolly Green Giant'll pick me up, he thought, passing in and out of consciousness. His eyes snapped open. I'm a Jolly Green Giant pilot. I can't be picked up. I pick up people!

It was confusing why he should be picked up and not be picking up other pilots.

Something's wrong, his mind warned. God! The pain!

He managed to open the Syrette of morphine and give himself an injection in the leg.

Pain racked his body and he felt himself fade in and out.

Chuck did not fully come to when the Filipino Medevac people got to him. Everything was a haze in his mind. But he was calm. For some reason, he knew these were friendlies and not the VC. God! I couldn't stand another go at that, he thought as he remembered being a POW again.

He felt no pain when they cut his leg off at the knee to free him from the tangled wreckage of the Apache.

They took out Captain Castello's body. Castello would never fly again or serve under the flag of the Philippines.

Truck kept his station over Chuck and the wrecked Apache until the Medevac had come and gone. When he saw that no NPA would try to get to the downed helicopter, he felt the classified computers in the craft were safe. If he felt the helicopter was in danger of being taken over by the NPA, he would have fired into the chopper to destroy it.

He flew off to do battle.

Jumper saw Chuck and Castello go down. "Ya bastards. That's good men ya shot down!"

He flew into the blazing fire of the M1939. Green fireflies whizzed toward him as he held on station while the gunner sighted in on the antiaircraft weapon, passing all around his aircraft. The copilot/gunner got a good sight picture and pressed the button. Rounds of 30-millimeter ammo from the chain gun flew straight and true to the antiaircraft weapon. The enemy gun stopped firing and started to disintegrate as the rounds hit with small explosions.

"Now, ya bastards, suck on that!" yelled Jumper. He had killed the gun that shot down Chuck, but he did not know if his friend had been saved or not.

Two down out of four. That's not very good odds, his mind growled.

He turned his Apache to join Red Dog to do more battle. He called into the radio, "Red Dog, you got a new wing man."

"Welcome aboard. Now stop talking and start shootin'."

Bo flew low over the battlefield. He and his spotter called in targets for the Apaches. After the ground force was committed, they called in targets for their mortars and for the soldiers to attack. When they saw targets they could attack, they flew low and dropped out mortar rounds. They made hits with the inopportune bombing.

Small-arms rounds hit the wings and fuselage of the small aircraft.

He checked his fuel. Damn! He would be running on fumes to make it to the camp.

Bo landed the plane just as it stuttered and the prop stopped turning. He coasted as far as he could.

Men ran out to the aircraft and pushed it to the refueling pump.

He ran out of fuel one time in Laos and had to leave his Bird Dog behind. Another Raven had picked him up. They returned with two cans of gas and luckily the old aircraft was still waiting for him. They fueled the Dog up and he took off just before the North Vietnamese regulars arrived.

The old air warrior got out of the airplane on stiff legs. He had been sitting in the cramped quarters of the small fixed-winged plane for hours. He could barely walk. He would not admit that middle age had anything to do with it. When he was younger, he could sit in a plane all day with little or no ill effects.

"Let's get ready," Bo told him. He hobbled around the Bird Dog with a roll of green GI "hundred mile an hour" tape, placing patches over holes in the wings and fuselage.

Men started bringing cases of mortar rounds and placing them beside the Bird Dog.

The spotter came up to the plane carrying a box of mortar rounds, followed by others with more rounds.

"Goddamn! We ain't gonna be able to get off the ground with this many," said Bo, laughing. He took the cup of tea handed him and downed the hot drink. "Take some of 'em outta the case and let's stack 'em near both seats."

This done, Bo got back inside the airplane and buckled up.

The young spotter grinned at his friends and crawled aboard. He was ready for more of the glory Bo was giving both of them. Bo had already become a hero to these young men.

Bo cranked the engine, brought up the RPM, kicked off the brakes, and shot down the runway. He was in the air before he had used up a third of the airstrip.

"It's back to war and glory," Bo said to no one in particular.

Back on station, Bo flew low, and he and the spotter both spent their time arming and dropping 60mm mortar rounds on the objective.

He flew up high for a look around. Philippine Air Force F-5A Freedom Fighters were making strikes on targets where the other ground forces were attacking. From the radio traffic, it seemed that the other forces were doing well.

A round hit the bottom of the Bird Dog behind Bo's seat. The spotter in the backseat gave out a yelp. The bullet from an old U.S.-made Garand rifle hit the bottom of the man's foot, drove through the top boot, and out the roof of the airplane.

Bo called, "You hit?"

"Bad! In the foot!" the scared man called out.

"You'll live. But we need more fuel anyway," replied Bo. He called over the air, "Bo Peep, off station for refuel. Out."

Bo flew back to the base and landed. The refueling crew came running out to service the airplane and get it back into the air.

"Get this man out of here! He's been hit!" called Bo.

Men ran to the plane and opened the door. They lifted the wounded spotter out of the plane and carried him away.

"I need another spotter," Bo informed the men.

"I be it," a young lieutenant called with a grin.

"Climb aboard, young trooper, and bring along some more mortar rounds," Bo instructed him.

The plane was topped off with fuel. The ground crew ran around the aircraft with tape, patching holes as Bo had done. Bo remained in the airplane, waiting for them to finish.

The new spotter finished loading the mortar rounds and got his restraint belt buckled up just as Bo was cranking up the O-1. He took off, ready for another go at this business.

Once off the ground, he patted the dash of the old Bird Dog. "You're as good as the old C-47. May we both hang in there together."

19

The trees on top of the mountains were not as tall or as thick as on lower elevations. The rangers used this lack of tree height to rappel from the helicopters to the ground behind Skull's emplacements. Heavier equipment and supplies were let down to the troops.

Hombros quickly formed up his men and moved forward. He planned to attack with two elements, with ten men in each element, and his third element would be reserves. The captain hoped to be on his objective by daylight.

Willie approved of the plan of attack. The old trooper knew it was going to be a tough fight with this small number of men, but sometimes in a surprise attack made by good men with strong air and artillery support, a unit could rout an enemy three times its size. The instructors at infantry school were not always right when they said that an attacking unit needed two to three times as many men as the defensive force. He and Meo tribesmen had beaten larger units in Laos. Also the Filipino rangers were not attacking a well-trained military force. The NPA was filled with inexperienced people that had only the desire, but not the training. He just hoped Truck and the Apaches killed the hell out of the enemy and had softened up the target.

Lieutenant Gutierrez grinned at Willie. Willie had become pretty close to the young lieutenant. The lieutenant was going to visit Willie and his wife after this was over. The old sergeant major would like to have a young army officer around him to instruct in being a better leader of troops.

Bad Bear waited until the ground attack force neared the fort before diving in to hit the enemy from the rear. He and Crackers had gone to the rear to refuel while the troops were moving into the attack position.

Crackers followed him down, picking out targets as he swept down upon the emplacements.

Bad Bear sent three rockets into the top of a bunker. He flew up and over the enemy positions, flying into the zone of the other attacking Apaches. He was signaled by the other aircrafts' computers that he was flying into a danger zone. He spun the Apache around and circled to the rear of the emplacements, firing into bunkers and trenches as he flew past.

A team of NPA men set up a light machine gun on the top of a bunker. The gunner jacked a round into the chamber and fired at the oncoming machine of death.

Rounds from the NPA machine gun bounced off the helicopter and were swatted down by the whirring prop. Bad Bear wished the enemy had a larger weapon to fight with so that the battle would be more evenly matched.

He signaled his gunner, who had ducked at the enemy's first burst, to blast away. One burst of the chain gun cleared the top of the bunker, killing men and destroying the gun.

He could have overridden the gunner and fired himself, but he needed to get the young Filipino back into action.

Bad Bear and Crackers swept the area with their guns and rockets.

A SAM missile flew past Bad Bear's helicopter, missing the Apache by ten feet. The young copilot in the front seat crossed himself and thanked his protector.

Crackers saw the team with shoulder-fired SAMs getting ready to fire another missile at Bad Bear. He signaled and the gunner fingered the button for a burst from the chain gun. Men and weapons disintegrated from the blast of the missile as it exploded on the shoulder of one of the men.

"Thanks heaps, little brother," Bad Bear told Crackers.

There was less and less resistance from the entrenchments of the NPA. Many had been killed by the air attack of the helicopters and others had gone underground, hoping that they could survive the onslaught. Many other NPA warriors were seen escaping to the flanks and down the sides of the mountain. They had never expected anything like this. They had had enough.

A noisy dawn crept into the noisy world. The sun seemed to edge up over the horizon to see if it was safe to show its face. Another war had awakened the countryside of these mountains that had been so quiet and peaceful since the brutal Japanese forces had left the Philippines many years ago.

Hombros looked at the new sun. He would have light to maneuver his forces and to see the enemy. He ordered the attack.

The attack force moved to the objective under the blanket of fire and smoke. Hombros went with one attack element, while Willie went with Lieutenant Gutierrez and the second element.

The attacking force received very little opposition. The enemy was not expecting an attacking force from the rear. Skull assured them that it would be impossible. So much for Skull's expertise in the field of military warfare and tactics.

The rangers jumped into the open trench network and started going from bunker to bunker, clearing them of armed personnel and weapons. Some of the fighting was hand to hand. They would throw hand grenades down into tunnels as they found their entrances. The NPA guerrilla soldiers had no chance against the Filipino rangers, an elite unit of handpicked men trained in this type of warfare.

Big Willie Falloure jumped into the trench and started firing and hitting men with his rifle. His size alone was intimidating. His yells of joy of battle, his barking rifle, and charging tactics made the young enemy guerrillas run for their lives. He came to a young guerrilla hiding behind a stack of ammunition boxes. The old sergeant major slapped the man in the face with his rifle barrel and then grabbed him and broke his neck as if it were a stick.

Willie moved to a bunker, juiced up on adrenaline for the kill.

A young NPA guerrilla swung his rifle toward Willie. Willie was still fast in his middle years. He fired from the hip and killed the young man before he could squeeze off a round. The second man dropped his rifle and started to raise his hands when he was hit by a blast from a ranger's rifle firing full automatic.

"I think ya was kinda slow, little boy," Willie said to the dead enemy.

Another burst came from the ranger beside Willie. Willie jumped to a fighting stance, ready to do or die.

The ranger pointed to an opening that led to a tunnel.

Willie walked to the hole and saw a Communist guerrilla lying in a heap on the floor of the tunnel. He pulled the pin on a grenade and pitched it far back into the tunnel. Willie turned and gave a thumbs-up to the younger ranger, who grinned back at him.

The fire team moved to another bunker and cleared it of enemy. No one was allowed to surrender in this bunker, either.

"These people don't like taking prisoners," Willie muttered to himself with a grin.

They moved down the trench, ever ready for a hidden enemy. They came to another bunker.

Willie moved up to the opening. A young NPA trooper stuck his head out to see if the enemy was coming his way. Willie slammed him in the face with the barrel of his M-16. The man let out a sigh and fell to the ground. Willie stepped in and fired a burst. The bunker was already cleared, the defenders leaving the sinking ship behind.

They moved down the trench to another bunker and halted.

Gutierrez joined them and pitched a high-explosive hand grenade through the open entrance. The explosion was muffled, indicating that it had rolled into a grenade trap.

"Willie, follow me!" called Gutierrez.

Willie followed Gutierrez into the bunker. Five men turned to face the rangers. The grenade had done no damage to the men inside the bunker, but they had been stunned by the concussion and were still trying to blink their eyes open.

Three immediately saw that their demise was upon them if they resisted. They laid down their weapons without firing a shot.

One of the men raised his rifle to fire, but was killed by the quick action of Willie and Gutierrez.

The fifth man fired a burst from his submachine gun, hitting the ceiling of the bunker above Willie. The man ran to the hole leading to the underground tunnel system. Willie fired his M-16 from the hip. Two rounds hit the man, one round in his leg and another in his right side. The wounds were not fatal.

"That's Skull!" called Gutierrez.

The Filipino lieutenant limped over to Skull and butt-stroked him with the butt of his M-16. He then dragged the fallen Communist leader to the center of the bunker. He looked up at the three men and asked, "Is this not Commander Skull?"

All three quickly nodded their heads that it was indeed he.

"Have you been hit?" asked Willie. He had noticed the lieutenant's limp.

Gutierrez shook his head, negative.

Willie checked him over and found a small hole in the calf of his left leg. The 9mm bullet had entered, but it had not exited. "Ya got hit in the leg."

"I don't feel anything."

"You will," Willie assured him.

Gutierrez called Hombros over the radio, "Captain, we have Skull. I repeat, we have Skull. He has been wounded—severely. You had better get here before he dies. Come east down the trench and you will find us."

The lieutenant called in a sergeant and three of his men to remove the three prisoners.

Hombros joined Gutierrez and Willie.

Gutierrez went to Skull and grabbed him by the hair. He jerked his head up for Hombros to take a look at him. Skull twisted and squirmed in obvious pain.

"Yes, that is the man who calls himself Skull," replied Hombros. "Well, Casto, I have finally caught up with you. I have not seen you since you killed those three women and two children five years ago."

"That was not me," groaned Skull through tight lips.

"Oh, yes, it was you. You are good at killing women and children," mocked the captain. "I hear that you rape little boys as well as little girls. You are indeed a pig."

"I am innocent of all charges," complained Skull. "It was not I who killed the women and children."

"Oh, yes. I saw you escaping. It was I who killed the two men you left behind as rear guard. I killed them and would have gone after you, but I was shot in the leg and could not follow. I still have a huge scar from that encounter. I was a lieutenant then. I swore that one day I would have you in my sights. When I got you in my sights, I told myself, I would kill you. I didn't care what the circumstances were at the time, I would kill you for all my men and friends you had killed," Hombros informed the Communist leader. The captain gave an evil grin. "Now is the time."

"What are you going to do?" Skull asked, gasping.

"Ask you a question. Where is Ybarra and his children?"

"I do not know," Skull told him. "Honestly. He was captured on my orders, but I do not know where they hold him. I did not order the pig to take the children as hostage."

"You were the one who ordered him to abduct Ybarra. Anything he does is your responsibility. Where is he?" barked Hombros.

"I do not know were he holds them," groaned Skull.

Hombros knew he would get nothing out of Skull even if he knew anything. One guerrilla usually did not know what the other one was doing. He growled, "I don't think my country needs you any longer. Now you're going to pay for your crimes against our people."

"What are you going to do?" asked Skull.

"Kill you. We don't need another prisoner to escape from prison after a lenient judge gives him a short sentence. You may escape and start an uprising where more of our people will die, for no more reason except to satisfy your small ego," said Hombros with an evil grin.

"You can't do this. It's against the law!" shouted Skull.

"On this mountain there is no law, except my law," growled Hombros. "Your law died with your guerrilla movement against my country and my people."

The Filipino captain noticed Willie standing in the bunker. The captain asked, "My friend, could you wait outside the bunker for me and the lieutenant?"

Without a pause, Willie answered, "I'd be glad to, Captain."

He stepped out of the bunker. A short moment later, he heard one pistol shot. Now he knew why Gutierrez announced over the air that Skull had serious wounds and may die of them.

"Skull has been killed in combat while we were trying to take his bunker," Hombros told Willie when he came outside. The captain lit a cigarette.

"You make the reports, Captain," said Willie. He pointed to the cigarette and said, "You know, those things'll kill ya, dead."

Willie keyed the radio. There was a slight smile on his lips when he called Truck over the air. "Attention C-and-C ship. Commander Skull has been killed in the battle. There is no leader for the Communist forces. I repeat, Commander Skull has been killed in the battle."

"Roger that. Out," returned Truck. He looked at Reyes and told him over the intercom. "We have a loudspeaker on this bird. Why don't you do a little reporting to the NPA troops?"

Reyes nodded his head in agreement. He flicked on the switch and called into the mike, "Attention! Attention! Commander Skull is dead. You are without a leader. I repeat, Commander Skull is dead. You are without a leader.

Stop your resistance immediately. Stop fighting government forces and lay down your arms. You will be taken and treated as prisoners of war."

Truck flew up and down the enemy lines while Reyes announced the news on the loudspeaker. They took a few small-arms rounds, but nothing serious.

The death of Skull was also reported to Peña and he gave the report to the NPA forces in the area. All resistance ceased and men started either running or throwing down their arms.

Firing slowly stopped on Skull's mountain fort and men started coming out of trenches and bunkers with their hands up. They did not know their fate at the hands of the government, but they knew that continued resistance would be fatal.

Rangers jumped into the trenches to clear them of all NPA guerrillas. The fighting was over.

Truck looked at his watch. It read 1003 hours. The fighting had lasted six hours. It had seemed longer, but in reality, it was a short fight. Guerrilla activities doing guerrilla things was one thing, but every time a guerrilla unit decided to face a hard-core professional army, they always got the short end of the stick. Most guerrilla forces did not have the training or the equipment to face a regular army in a conventional fight.

"I'm hungry," Truck said to no one in particular.

The news of Skull's death spread over the mountains. Peña also reported for the NPA benefit that the government was already sending out troops in truck convoys to clear the mountain strongholds of all enemies of the people. Surrender was the best and smartest choice. Death was inevitable for those who did not surrender.

The Filipino rangers started mopping up and taking

prisoners in the outlying areas of Skull's mountain fort. Most of the dispirited NPA members surrendered without firing a shot. Many of the guerrillas took to the mountains and escaped. Most would find their way back to their homes. Some would remain in the mountains and become bandits. That was the usual vocation of the hard core who would not give up to government authorities. They would wait for some other leader to come forth, spewing his Communist brand of ideology.

It was a good day for the people and government of the Philippines. The people were slowly realizing that the problem was not just a government one. They, the people, were the government. If they were indeed the government, then it was their problem as well.

The Apaches flew back to their base and after a quick check and servicing by the ground crews, they were pushed back under the shed to keep them from view.

Push immediately went to work, correcting any defect or damage done in the fight.

It was hoped that word of the flying tanks would be considered an overstatement by the NPA guerrillas. That would make it easier.

If the world did learn about the helicopters, the report would be that a special team of contract men were working with the Philippine government. This team was obeying the laws of the United States and giving aid and assistance to the Philippine government as directed by the president. That would not quiet Congress or the press, but it would make them have to search for a better lead story.

20

Truck walked across the compound to Peña's headquarters.

Peña looked up and smiled at Truck. "Welcome, my friend. We have made a good fight together, eh?"

"That we have," agreed Truck.

"We have done our part, now the people in the rear can do their part," said Peña.

The U.S. commander of Clark Air Force Base sent a recovery team to retrieve the wreckage of Chuck's downed Apache. They would also search the area for the remains of The Gooch's downed helicopter. The air force people would take the wreckage back to the secret hangar and return it to the United States.

"That pilot you called The Gooch, he was one tough *hombre*, eh? He blew that thing up and took many with him," Peña said admiringly.

From the type of blast that destroyed the Apache, there was no doubt that he had blown the helicopter himself.

"Yeah, that's a fact in war when hot lead starts flying.

The brave and the good die right along with the cowards and the bad," returned Truck.

"What about the man you called Chuck? What of him?" asked Peña.

"He has lost his right leg. His left leg was broken, and so were some ribs. There was no back injury or head injury. There were some internal injuries that will be a problem. He is being sent back to Hawaii to Tripler Hospital. He is on active duty and will be retired as a disabled navy officer," Truck told him. He hoped the navy would promote him to the rank of full captain when they gave him his retirement. He thought SOCOM would see to that.

"What do you do now?" asked Peña.

"We're taking the Apaches back to Clark. Then I've got to go to the States and report to my people," Truck told him. He knew Peña wondered what the team was going to do after this, but he was not going to go any further with the conversation. "Your people did very well. They were professionals. We all, every one of us, were honored that we could assist the people of the Philippines."

"Thank you. You honor me and my men greatly," replied Peña with a pleased voice. It was indeed an honor to be praised by a man such as Truck Grundy. He was an old warrior who had been in many wars and many battles. He would know good men and a good unit when he saw one. "You will not return to Clark today, will you?"

"No. I have requested that we wait until tomorrow morning. Then we will all move at once," replied Truck.

"Tonight we will have a special meal to honor our American friends. Women and booze will flow tonight, believe me," Peña said with a smile.

Truck thanked him and went to the barracks that housed the Americans. He told the team, "Tonight Peña wishes to give us a going-away meal and drinking party. What say you boys?"

The remaining members of the team looked at each other. They had lost one dead, and another one was severely wounded.

Finally, Red Dog spoke up. "I say we go. That crazy wild man, Gooch, would have a real, goddamned mad-on if we didn't go."

"That's for a fact," agreed Jumper.

"I'm ready to drink to his departure," said Bad Bear. "He will be in our brigade in the Afterworld, waiting, when we all get there."

"Then it's done," said Truck, walking off to his room. He stopped and turned back to the men. "Tonight is our last night with these people. They're gonna bring women. If any of 'em suits your fancy, I'm sure you'd honor our brother soldiers by screwing their women."

"Well, goddamn! Old Truck is human, after all," said Jumper, laughing.

"He knows. He was a big stud in his younger days," Bad Bear answered with a grin.

Without looking back, Truck shot him the "bird."

Mano looked up at the sky. He had been watching the airplanes search for him and the others all day. But now his eyesight had become a blur and he could only hear the aircraft.

God, I hurt! his mind screamed. He groaned out loud.

He heard a small, single-engine airplane fly overhead. He tried to dig into the hard ground to hide himself.

Every bare area of his skin was covered with mosquito bites and bites from the many insects that inhabit the jungles of the Philippines. Bites from army ants had already become small festering spots. There were leeches digging into his flesh under his clothing. One stung him in the crack of his ass and he could not dig it loose with his one good hand. His left hand and arm were useless from being shattered by a round from an American M-16 bullet.

His clothes were covered with mud and they had not dried. He was thirsty and hungry. The men who deserted him had taken all of the food and water with them. They were poor peasants who had learned long ago to look out for themselves. That was the way their kind survived in this land.

Mano had been with the attack force that attacked Clark Air Force Base. He had lost nearly all of the men and women attackers who had been with him. As they pulled back, a unit, from which army he did not know, struck the remaining guerrillas in the flank. That was the last of his unit. People died, surrendered, or fled into the jungle.

Four men had escaped with Mano. One was severely wounded and they finally left him behind to die alone. His continuous crying out in pain would give all of them away. Sacrifice one to save the others.

The three men had grown tired of carrying Mano and, taking everything, including all weapons, they had left him to die alone.

It was hot and Mano was more miserable than he had ever been in his life. He never thought things were going to be like this. He had hopes of the glory and success of the movement. He was idealistic in his thoughts and actions and was a true follower of the Maoist doctrine.

He tried to look down at his stomach wound. His eyes were swollen and everything had become a blur. He knew he was dying. Nothing could possibly hurt this badly and let him live through it.

"Oh, God, I tried!" he gasped out loud.

He had tried what? To better the people's lives? To gain

a new government for the people? Or had he hoped only for power for himself? He did not know.

The wound in his stomach started to sting so badly that it brought tears to his eyes. He pulled back his blood-soaked shirt and tried to see the wound. His eyes finally focused and he saw a leech feeding on the open wound. It slowly crawled deeper into the wound, making him scream louder.

"Oh, my God! Mother, mother, I miss you so much!" cried the defeated guerrilla.

Pain swept over him and he passed into a deep, silent darkness.

Peña set up the meal in the small officers' mess. It was filled to capacity with the influx of officers, "ladies," and senior sergeants.

After the meal, Peña toasted the Americans. The Filipinos stood to drink in honor of their allies.

Peña produced patches and insignias of the army's First Scout Rangers, the air force's Air Commandos, and the marines' Special Operations teams, all of whom the Eagle Attack Team had worked with. They were presented to each American. Peña told the Americans, "We are honored to present these to our friends and brother soldiers."

Truck spoke for all of them and said, "We have found, as we always have, that professional soldiers always speak the same language and are honorable men. We are proud to be among professional soldiers."

With the formalities over, the group started doing some serious drinking.

A group of Filipinos were trying to match Bad Bear up in a wrestling match with a huge ranger sergeant. Bad Bear was not interested. He had what he wanted. It had a skirt and a low-cut blouse to exposed prominent, firm breasts.

"How about an arm-wrestling match?" called Crackers.

"What?" questioned the Filipinos. They looked at each other.

"Ah, yes. I've seen Americans do it. Their sailors love the arm wrestling," a man put in.

"No," growled Red Dog. "I ain't in the mood."

"For money, ya ain't in the mood?" asked Crackers.

"No."

"For glory of the team, ya ain't in the mood?"

"Hell no."

"Well I'll be goddamned!" exploded Crackers. He was always looking out for ways to keep his purse full.

"You'll be more than that if ya start on me," exclaimed Red Dog calmly.

"Uh-huh. I'm scared of you quiet guys," commented Crackers. Then he called to the Filipino rangers and air commandos, "I guess you guys'll have to fight among yourselves."

They took his word on it and a ranger sergeant knocked an air force commando sergeant out a window. The fighting started and Peña called out, "Cease this right now!"

No one heard him, or at least continued as if they had not.

Peña walked out of the club to an armed guard. He took the young soldier's rifle and returned to the club. Inside, he pointed the rifle into the air and fired into the ceiling. The rifle was on full automatic and a line of bullet holes was left in the ceiling.

The noise of the rifle firing full automatic stopped the fighting. Men ran in from the outside to see what was happening.

Peña looked up at the ceiling. He did not crack a smile or frown in anger when he said, "All, and I mean all, ranger and air commando sergeants will start repairing the roof at dawn in the morning. There will be no assistance from the enlisted men. Only sergeants will work on the roof."

The men stood, looking from the colonel to the ceiling.

The sergeant major roared, "Tomorrow morning there will be a formation of all NCOs in this camp. Even those who were not at the party will be in the formation. We will work on the officers' mess roof. I will be the supervisor. If anyone falls off the roof, he will not be excused from the work site until the repair is finished. Am I understood?"

"Yes, Phuong Sarhento!" a unison of voices cried.

"Now let's party until we must go to work," the sergeant major ordered. The sergeant major turned to Peña and saluted sharply. He picked up his drink and stood, smiling.

"By God, you do have a bunch of fine men, Colonel," said Willie.

"May one sergeant major buy another sergeant major a drink?" asked a pleased Filipino sergeant.

"I'd be glad and honored to drink with you," replied Willie.

"I know a woman who I think would satisfy any sergeant major," exclaimed the Filipino.

"Well, I sure would like to be satisfied," replied Willie as the two men walked off.

Red Dog looked Peña over approvingly. "I gotta admit, you're my type of soldier."

"Thank you very much, sir," returned Peña. "A man must be firmly in charge. But not too firmly."

This brought smiles.

"I sure wish I had a boss like that," sighed Crackers.

No one was interested in listening to him.

Peña and Truck walked off to one side. Peña told him, "I have been told that the NPA is breaking up for now. I don't mean it's destroyed, but that it will stick to guerrilla activities and murder of our people by terrorist acts. Skull just about broke the movement's back when he made that stupid abduction. The people may not have liked him attacking the U.S. military bases, but that would not have angered them against the CPP and NPA. But their abducting children, and the word being put out that this pig, the so-called Aguerrido, holding them was a sex pervert who assaulted small girls—well, that was the back breaker."

"I'm always glad to see a sex pervert, or any other kind of pervert, put completely out of the ranks of mankind," growled Truck. "Maybe your people will catch him and send him to join Skull and his kind."

"Let us hope that will be so," said Peña.

The party went on until formation call was sounded for the camp's NCOs at 0800 hours. The Filipino sergeant major stood in front of the formation in fatigues, ready to go to work. The sergeants stood in the formation in different types and parts of uniforms. They were also in different modes of sobriety.

When the order was given, the sergeants hauled out ladders and equipment and climbed upon the roof. One fell down the ladder, and one fell off the roof. Their only medicine was another drink from the bottle.

Young enlisted men sat outside the officers' mess and bar, amazed that all of their sergeants were working so hard and that they had not been requested to join them. They did not know why the sergeants were working on the roof. Word was spread around that it had to do with something that happened last night, like a rifle going off and punching holes in the roof.

Bad Bear looked at the sergeants repairing the roof in the heat of the early morning. He took note of the enlisted men, sitting around and pointing with laughter at their sergeants. He told Truck, "You know, boss, I bet that colonel boosted morale in this camp a hundred percent by that order."

Truck smiled. "I bet you're right."

The men climbed into the Apaches and Hueys and flew off.

The roof of the officers' mess was covered with men when the Eagle Attack Team flew out of the camp and back to Clark. The sergeants waved at the aircraft and held bottles skyward.

21

The team spent the next few days after returning to Clark cleaning and repairing equipment.

Headquarters at Bragg sent a classified message that a technical representative from McDonnell Douglas and a team of military mechanics were on their way to the Philippines. Their only mission was to get the helicopters back into number-one flying condition as soon as possible.

The men in the team were glad to hear that news. They wondered how long they were going to be left at Clark. They were sure they would not have long to sit around with Truck bossing this team.

Willie went home to his wife and to make a visit to the hospital to see Lieutenant Gutierrez.

The McDonnell Douglas tech rep and mechanics from the States arrived at the base. They immediately went to work.

Push came to Truck with a report. "This bunch brought

a basic load of ammo with 'em of everything except Hellfire missiles. I suppose they are holding those in reserve."

Truck shrugged his shoulders. "What'd the tech rep say about the choppers?"

"He said they were in good shape. They went through the battle and didn't receive any major damage. Their job is gonna be as much cosmetic as anything else."

"Thanks," said Truck. He walked over to the coffeepot and poured another cupful.

Push returned to watch over his pets.

Colonel Ramos called Truck and asked if he would come to Fort Bonifacio for a visit. Truck was agreeable and was sent the same hard-body sedan he used before. The NPA may have been set back, but the CPP assassination squads, called "sparrows," were still in operation.

The same lieutenant aide and driver were sent. They talked as much this time on the trip into Manila as they did the first time—which was none.

"Ah, Truck Grundy, my friend," General Ruiz greeted them when Truck walked into his office.

"General. Colonel," Truck greeted Ruiz and Ramos as he walked into his office.

"You and your men did such an outstanding job. We of the Philippines will forever be in your debt. I only wish we could hold a parade and show you the honor and respect of which you are deserving," said the general.

Truck smiled. He had been in covert work for many years and had to settle for private praise and no public show of decorations and parades after the mission was completed. He always liked a parade. A parade with a big marching band would have him come running ever since he was a boy in Texas. Truck said, "General, putting Skull out of action was satisfaction enough for both me and my men."

Ramos grinned. "I understand Peña gave you a good farewell dinner."

Truck laughed with them. "They're a good bunch of men. Both professionally as well as personally. They're my kind of people. They're the kind you need when you're in trouble. I hope the people and government of the Philippines realize that and take it into consideration when praise is sent out."

"Yes, it will be remembered," the general assured him. "With men like Ramos here to keep us straight, we will remember. Flaco Ramos spent many years in the bush with troops before he came here to live like a human. He was one of the good commanders we were able to promote when the present government came into power. We have gained much advice from him in antiterrorist activities. Before our president came along, many of the best commanders were left in the bush to spend a lifetime fighting for a country that did not care. Only Marcos's cronies rose in rank. Those of us who were promoted and were not Marcos's favorites were lucky."

"We called men such as you 'token' promotions," said Ramos honestly.

"We were that," admitted Ruiz.

An aide brought in hot tea for all of them.

"What about this abduction of Ybarra? Have you found him and his children yet?" asked Truck.

"No. But we still believe he is somewhere in greater Manila. The National Bureau of Investigation and our Intelligence Service are working together to find the place where they're held," General Ruiz informed him. "We only hope they are all alive."

"I only hope we can get into the safe house and not get all of them killed," said Ramos.

General Ruiz looked at him sharply. He should not be

saying such things to an outsider, even if it was such as this American.

Ramos saw the look and said, "General, that is so. And I have a plan to get them out alive. We will force the local police to use our people. With the training Peña told me his people received under our friends, I am sure they can get into the safe house."

"You mean this Phoenix-type training?" asked Ruiz.

"Yes, General. Hombros has informed me that he has the men trained to enter safe houses. They were trained by Bad Bear and Willie. Most of our people are still learning such tactics," Colonel Ramos told the general.

The general called for more tea. He sat, waiting.

"Let me call Hombros in. He can help in this project," urged Ramos.

"There will be a jurisdiction fight with the bureau," said Ruiz.

"Then so be it, General. Tell the president we can use some of her powers under martial law," Ramos reminded him. "And for the benefit of our country, we had better do all we can to get Ybarra and his children back alive. Especially his children. The people will not stand a government that will not move to protect innocent children."

General Ruiz thought a moment and then he said, "Let it be done."

"I'll do that while you and Truck visit," said Ramos, getting up from his chair and leaving the office.

"That is one good man," said Ruiz.

"I agree," added Truck.

The two men made a short visit. Before Truck left, he asked, "How do you think your country will go in renewing our base leases?"

"I think it will go well. Our government has slowly been able to convince people that with the United States bases here in our country, we can have external security while we are handling our internal problems," General Ruiz told Truck. "It is now being said that we can even handle our internal problems with the American bases present in our country. I think the people will demand that the Senate vote for renewal of the leases."

"That's what I wanted to know," said Truck, flashing a grin. He saluted and left the office.

The lieutenant held the sedan door open when he got outside. The car shot forward as the lieutenant was closing his door.

Truck got the team together. "I have been called back to the States. I'll leave Tuesday. Do any of you want to go home for a leave?"

The men looked at each other.

"Ya know, boss, I don't think any of us have a home," said Bad Bear. "I mean, old Chuck was the only one who had a wife and family waiting for him. I don't know for sure about the rest of the men, but I don't. I'd just as soon stay here and wait for our next assignment, for wherever Uncle Sam sends us next."

"As long as my scotch holds out I'm satisfied here in the Philippines," was all Red Dog had to say.

"What about Nancy?" Truck asked.

Red Dog growled, "She don't need me, I don't need her."

"I done got kicked outta my home. The booze and the women are all just fine in the Philippines," put in Jumper.

"I get married every night and divorced every morning," said Crackers. "I mean, hell, four times before a judge should tell me something."

"Yeah, that you can't hold a woman," said Jumper, and laughed.

The rest of the team joined him in the laughter.

"Like the rest of ya can, huh?" returned Crackers.

They already knew Bo's circumstances. They looked at Push.

"That's the reason I'm here. My wife took my sons and daughter back to Hawaii," said Push. "I would like to get back home and see my kids and the old people once in a while. Other than that, I go where you and those Apaches go."

"Then take a trip to Hawaii and see your family. Kids need to see their dad as often as possible," said Truck. Where had he heard that one before?

"I'll do that, Colonel," promised Push.

"Ain't we a poor bunch? Only Willie has someone waiting for him," said Truck, shaking his head. "Well, for now, I suggest we go into Manila and visit Panther."

"I'll put a second on that and call for questions," said Crackers quickly.

"I'm already on my way in," said Bo, putting on a fresh shirt. He waved as he walked out the door.

Everyone agreed to going into town, except Push. Push wanted to stay behind and not leave his aircraft to others. He told his friends, "I want to be sure that all my choppers fly the way they're supposed to. I do that by making sure they're taken care of properly."

"Push, those guys know their job. Hell, let 'em do their duty while we do ours—gettin' drunk and gettin' laid," said Crackers, laughing.

"You've been the hardest-working one in the bunch, Push. I think it's time for a break. Go in with us and enjoy yourself," urged Truck.

"Well, I might go in, but I ain't gonna enjoy myself," said Push.

"The clean-living all-American boy," grinned Jumper.

"No, I just want my choppers to fly like they're supposed to," Push informed him, heading for the shower.

Truck led the team members into Panther Bar. Although two were lost and two others missing, six still made up a good-size team.

Willie, the seventh member, was already at the bar. Bo Peep Day, the eighth man, was now the only one missing.

Willie yelled, "Clear a table, the warriors have landed!"

Two guys sitting at a table took one look at Willie, then at the Eagle Attack Team, and offered them their table. Extra chairs were found to place seven around the table.

Panther raised a frail hand at the crew.

Truck walked over to Panther and sat down next to his wheelchair. "Business good, Panther?"

"Not bad. It's been damned good since that arm-wrestling match," Panther smiled. He took a drink from his glass and looked at Truck and asked, "That you boys that took the fort from the so-called Commander Skull?"

Truck returned with, "We did our part."

"I thought you was here for a reason. I never knew Truck Grundy to make a trip just for the hell of it," chuckled Panther. "Now, if I could get a motor and wings on this damned thing I'm riding in, I'd make a few trips with you."

Panther had been around a long time. It had not taken him long to figure out what had gone down. He knew the system and how it worked. Better still, he knew the men who made it work.

"Panther, it's highly classified, but we have equipment that is top of the line," was all Truck said.

Panther looked at him a moment. He said, "So the rumors the NPA is putting out are true. There are flying monsters."

Truck remained silent.

"You're a helicopter pilot as well as a damned good paratrooper and infantryman. But you're getting too old to beat the bush. So ya gotta be flying those things. There's only one flying machine that is a 'monster,' like they've been talking about. It's a helicopter and it's the tank killer AH-64 Apache built by McDonnell Douglas," Panther commented. He did not expect an answer from Truck. He knew his old friend was a "businessman" who did his job and went on about his business, not a blabbermouth who tried to impress people.

"They haven't located Ybarra and his children yet, last I heard?" asked Truck.

"Nope. Don't know if they will. You know this town. There's plenty of places to hide," Panther informed him. He looked over at the team's table. Girls had gathered around its members. "The word has gotten around that the big spenders are back in town."

Truck looked over at his men and grinned. "They deserve a good time."

"I hope those damned Sparrows are laying low," commented Panther.

Mary came over to the table and bent down to hug Truck. "Glad to see ya, Truck. Panther's been waiting on you to come in."

"Always, when I'm in the neighborhood," smiled Truck.

"The girls are swarming around your table," observed Mary. "Truck, you leave those girls alone. I have a friend I want you to meet. She is out of the business now, but she likes a good man around once in a while."

"Hell, Mary," Truck mumbled, a little embarrassment in his voice.

"Don't mumble to me, Truck Grundy. I'm a big girl. I know what you boys do when you walk out of here with one of those girls," Mary laughed. "This girl is not only pretty, she has her own money."

Panther grinned. "You know a woman can't stand to see a man that's not attached to some female. If she can't set you up with one on a permanent basis, she's at least got to fix you up for the weekend."

"Yeah, why is it a woman hates to see a man running fancy free?" asked Truck. He accepted another bottle of beer someone in the team bought.

"Because. A man isn't supposed to be running free. It's against nature, unless he's looking for something," insisted Mary.

A woman in her late thirties to early forties walked into the bar and looked around. When she saw Mary and Panther, she walked over to them.

"That's her," Mary told Truck.

She was a fine-looking woman. She looked like a mixture of Spanish and Filipino native, with a Chinese ancestor thrown in somewhere down the line. She was not hard looking, as were many of the street prostitutes. Mary had said she was one of the "nicer" girls, which meant she was not a street whore but a woman of higher price, whom only the rich tourists and Filipino businessmen could afford.

"Octavia, it is good of you to come," Mary greeted the woman, and hugged her. "Truck, this is Octavia. We came from the same village and went to school together."

"Octavia," Truck said in greeting.

"I am glad to meet you, Truck," she returned.

"And don't let this shy, tongue-tied man fool you. He is wild and doesn't have a woman to keep him tied down," said Panther with a laugh.

"He doesn't look too tame," admitted Octavia.

"Truck, we're gonna roam awhile and be back in a short while," called Crackers.

Crackers, Jumper, and Push left the bar with five girls. A young woman hung on to Push, whose face was flush from drink and excitement of the night to come. Push was doing his best not to enjoy himself.

Mary went back behind the bar, while Truck and Octavia joined Bad Bear, Red Dog, and Willie.

Truck introduced Octavia to the men and asked, "What you doing sitting here, Bear? You tired or something?"

"He's not tired. He's waiting on somebody," said Willie with a grin. "He told me he don't like big women no more."

Bad Bear ignored him.

Red Dog picked up his scotch and without a word walked up to the bar to find a seat and drink alone.

"Is he antisocial or something?" asked Octavia.

"No doubt about it, the man's something," Truck informed her.

Bo Peep walked into the bar with a young woman. The girl was no more than seventeen or eighteen years old.

"That's one of those seventeen-year-old girls I used to sober old Bo up," Willie informed them.

Bo joined them. He looked around the table and said, "No, she ain't my daughter or my niece."

No one said a word. Bo did not introduce the young girl to them. He ordered a Coke and she had a Sprite. He was on the wagon to stay, at least for a while.

The young woman that had taken Bad Bear home the last time came into the bar. When she saw the big Indian, she squealed and ran to jump in his lap. "Oh, my big man, you have come back to me."

Bad Bear was pleased, but his expression never changed.

"I think we should leave—right now," the woman announced.

"Not if I got to fight your husband and his brother again," Bad Bear told her.

"Oh, no. My husband is still in the hospital. His brother is a coward without my husband behind him." The woman laughed. "Besides, we don't go home this time."

Bad Bear stood up, put the woman down, and said, "I'll see ya, boss."

The two walked out the door.

Willie shook his head as he watched the pair. "You talk about a Mutt and Jeff! Man, she must be something to satisfy that big guy."

Truck looked at Octavia. He told her, "It's been a long time. Let's go right now."

Without a word, she got up and left. Truck followed her out the door.

Mary called to them, "I don't want to see you two before tomorrow night."

Bo and his girl left.

Willie looked around at the empty chairs and said, "Guys, I think I got a woman waiting for me at home."

The big black man got up, waved to all those interested, and left.

Red Dog was happy. He had his scotch, two girls were in an argument, and people left him alone.

It was a quiet night for the Eagle Attack Team, for a change.

22

Truck walked into the First Special Operations Command HQ at Fort Bragg, North Carolina. He went to General Olive's office. When Truck entered the general's outer office, the aide jumped up to greet him. The secretary buzzed the general's office. The aide opened the door and Dan was around his desk by the time Truck got into the room.

"Truck, it's good to see you," greeted Dan. He nodded to the aide that coffee was needed. "Let's sit. I'd like to hear it directly from you."

Once they got settled, Dan told Truck, "Come on, give me a short firsthand report."

Truck gave him a sketch of what had happened the past few weeks. He also had a good combat report to give on the AH-64, which everyone seemed to want.

"Yeah, I read the report that you sent a couple of days ago. General Sullivan has read it and is anxious to talk to you," put in Dan.

Truck finished the briefing and held up the empty cup for more coffee.

Dan filled it from the coffeepot and sat back down.

"You boys did a good job," Dan said with enthusiasm. "The Filipinos are happy. Most of all, our high muckedy-mucks are happy that no bad press came from this operation. The fallout from bad publicity would have scared this program out of existence."

"Yeah, I know, Dan. Some goddamned politician would be trying to tell me that the program had to be stopped for the good of our country," growled Truck. "In all honesty, and politicians ain't great for that, is that the program would be pulled so that some damned politician could remain in office. I'm getting kinda tired of those guys, and those who think they have all the morals of what our country should and should not do. Everyone I've heard shoot off their mouths about what our country should be doing and not doing have got their own personal or political agenda, and they're not worrying about my country."

"Your geared up, aren't you, Truck?" asked Dan with a smile.

"Yep," said Truck. "People in both those groups got me in a war in Korea that we had to stop half-finished. Then they got me involved in Southeast Asia, where we got good people involved and then walked off and left them to die from torture and starvation in reeducation camps. Yeah, I'm geared up, Dan."

"We'll do the best we can to keep this program going," Dan assured him.

Truck accepted a refill of coffee. Damn, this stuff is getting to my stomach, he told himself again for the millionth time. He said out loud, "Dan, this program is one of the best we have going. We're helping these economically poor countries do for themselves, not doing it for them. All we're doing is knocking out stuff they don't have the technical ability to do for themselves. That's what we were supposed to have been doing in Vietnam and Laos. We've got a chance now. Look what it's done this time. We may have gotten the U.S. a new lease on our bases in the Philippines. But most important of all, we helped them gain a little better hold on a democratic form of government. And, I repeat, I said *helped*, Dan, not did it for them or gave it to them. They're doing it themselves, that's what's important. You get some of our left-wing or right-wing politicians involved in foreign politics and things'll get screwed up every damned time. They'll get screwed up because the politicians will tell our people, 'Look, see what I've done for their people. Got them ten billion dollars to play with. By my actions, they are now a free people.' They'll take credit for anything that's happened in that country, or they'll back off and snipe at the other party if something gets screwed up. I can sure go the rest of my life without that."

Dan walked to his desk and got a report and brought it for Truck to read. It was a medical report on Chuck. He was going to be retired from the navy. Dan said the navy had informed him that Chuck would be retired in the grade of commander.

"What? Like hell!" spat Truck.

"I think the navy didn't have much use for him after he turned down that desk job and went with SOCOM. He's now out on his own, with no one to look after his interests," said Dan.

"Like hell he is," Truck barked out. "He's got one old beat-up, retired LTC Truck Grundy on his team."

"I thought you might say that," Dan said, grinning. "I got an appointment for me and you to go and see Sullivan. We leave here in about ten minutes."

"Has that fourth star made him into much of a politician?" asked Truck.

"He's changed. Most of us do the higher we get. We call it seeing the big picture," Dan told him.

"Bullshit!" Truck said dryly.

Dan grinned, and then asked, "You going to stop off and see Linn?"

"Yep, on my way back," admitted Truck. "I called her from Frisco. She said she had a new chute that I'd just fall in love with. Damn! I wish she'd fall in love with some young stud and give me a grandkid."

"Are you still jumping very often?" asked Dan.

"Yeah, every once in a while," admitted Truck. "These new square rigs they got nowadays, they're easy on old bones. You can come in on an easy standing landing every time, no matter if there's a little wind or something. They're not anything like the old T-7 and T-10. Anyone can jump these things."

"How long have you been jumping, Truck?"

"Since '49, I reckon. Jumped out of an old biplane in a sport parachute an old boy used in his barnstorming. That was one tough chute. Like to've split me in half, from the crotch up. All of them were tough until the T-10 came along. Parachuting started gettin' tame then."

"Let's walk over to the headshed," suggested Dan.

They got up and walked out of the office and building. The aide stepped in behind them, making sure that he did not get close enough to get into the conversation.

The sedan driver drove directly to Joint Special Operations Command Headquarters and parked the car.

The move of Joint Military SOCOM from McDill Air Force Base had angered many of the upper echelon of the military, but it placed all of the staff and headquarters of the main operational units within walking distance of each other. The biggest bulk of everyday forces of JMSOCOM were the U.S. Army Special Forces; the U.S. Army Ranger battalions; Delta Force; U.S. Navy Sea, Air, and Land teams; U.S. Air Force Commandos, and attached and support units. Also located at Fort Bragg were the 18th Airborne Corps, the 82nd Airborne Division, and corps and division support units. That meant there were enough generals to fill the parking lots with For Generals Only parking signs. A four-star general commanded the Joint Military SOCOM, with three or four other generals and admirals from all the services with ranks from three stars down to one. The 18th Airborne Corps was commanded by a three-star general with a one-star as chief of staff. The 82nd Airborne Corps was commanded by a two-star general with two one-star generals as assistant CGs. First SOCOM was commanded by a two-star general with one-star general as deputy. The Special Warfare Center and Special Forces were commanded by a two-star general. That made somewhere around twelve to fourteen flag-rank officers of four stars down to one star.

Dan walked into Sullivan's outer office and informed the aide that they had an appointment to see the general. The aide announced Dan and Truck and motioned them into the office.

"Well, well, Truck Grundy. I see you're still alive," greeted Sullivan, shaking Truck's hand.

"Unbelieved by most, but it's true."

"Do we need coffee in here?" asked Sullivan.

"Not me. I've had my quota," Truck told him.

Dan nodded that he agreed for no more coffee.

Sullivan motioned them to chairs around a low table. Sullivan was an old paratrooper. He had received his jump wings while he was still a cadet at West Point. He had served in airborne units as a junior officer and field-grade officer in his early career. He was also Special Forces qualified and had been the commanding general of the Special Warfare Center, the First SOCOM, the 18th Airborne Corps, and now the Joint Military SOCOM. He had been around special warfare and anti-guerrilla warfare most of his career. He made an extra effort to sound and act like a rough, gruff trooper.

"So you kicked ass and took names over in the Philippines," said Sullivan.

"We did our job," was Truck's only comment.

"You gave a good after-action report on the combat application, abilities, and how well the Apache stood up in combat," the general told him. "But some are wondering why you lost two of those choppers."

"It was in my report," said Truck. His one good eye looked directly into Sullivan's eyes. "If they can't read a report that is written and documented properly, I question their ability to be in a position of responsibility."

Sullivan looked at Dan and then back at Truck. "You haven't changed a goddamned bit.

"Okay, that's what I'll tell them in my next commander-and-staff meeting."

Dan spoke up. "General, we're here because Truck is concerned about Commander Charles Taylor not being retired from the navy as a captain."

"Dan said you would be in here raising hell about Taylor not making captain." Sullivan gave a dry smile.

"I hope I don't have to," said Truck. He again looked Sullivan in the eyes. "That is one good man. He knows his job, he did his job, and now the navy wants to fuck with him because he went SOCOM instead of staying with them and working in the Pentagon. That's wrong and it should be corrected."

"If he is not retired with the rank of captain, what are you going to do?" asked Sullivan.

"Contact the President of the United States and also the President of the Philippines. I know I'll get support from the Philippines. I don't know about our president."

Sullivan sat back, looking at Truck for a moment. "You'd do it, too, wouldn't you?"

"Does a paratrooper use a parachute?" Truck asked without a smile.

Sullivan cracked a slight smile and reached for the telephone on the table. He told his secretary, "Get me Chief of Naval Operations."

A few minutes passed and the secretary buzzed him back. "The chief is not in, but one of the staff officers is there."

"I've been talking to a Rear Admiral Purviance about Taylor. He's the new guy that we talk to in the Chief's office about navy personnel down here," Sullivan explained.

"Get me Admiral Purviance," Sullivan told the secretary. After a few moments, Sullivan said, "Admiral, this is Bryan Sullivan, CG of Joint SOCOM at Bragg. I've got a couple of men in my office who will listen in on the conversation. One of them is in command of a special team one of your men was on."

Sullivan punched the button to place the call on a speaker.

"What can I do for you, General?" asked Purviance.

"General Olive, who's here with me, has called you about a Commander Charles Taylor, who is assigned to a special team we have operating in Asia," Sullivan informed him. "We are concerned that Taylor is not going to be retired with the rank of captain."

"Yes, I have talked to Olive about this situation. It is true that Taylor is due to be placed on the captains' list, but he will be medically retired before the list comes out or just about that time," the voice of Purviance came over the telephone speaker. "His career branch feels that the promotion should be given to a man who will remain on active duty. Besides, we here at navy don't know exactly what Taylor was doing when he was injured."

Sullivan looked at Truck and Dan and went into his tough paratrooper act. "Well, Admiral, by God I can tell you what Taylor was doing. He was carrying out the duty he was assigned to do as a member of this command. And as a member of this command, he is going to be looked out after by this goddamned command."

There was a pause, then the voice said, "General, we in the navy have responsibility to look out after our people. That's what we will do. We will decide on who to promote and not promote in our branch of service."

Sullivan looked up with a grin. He was ready to do battle. "Well, I'll tell you what, Admiral. This president of ours is very interested in JMSOCOM. He knows that men from all the services are assigned to this command. As an old navy war veteran, it would chap his ass to find out that navy is not taking care of their people, because they're in a command that he supports. Then the second thing you got to worry about is me. I command this outfit. And I tell you this: if you people want the sailors you send down here to be treated equally with the other troops, you'd better goddamned well remember that I command this outfit the way I want to. I will continue to do so at the president's pleasure, and, by God, I got his pleasure."

Sullivan was enjoying himself.

"I wouldn't go off half-cocked, General," said Purviance.

"I don't need no sailor to tell me how to go off," Sullivan broke in. "Goddamnit, you consider what I just told you. You and the Chief talk it over if you have to. But if Taylor doesn't go out as a captain, then we down here will figure you people don't like us special operations folks.

"That's all, Admiral."

Sullivan punched the button, cutting Purviance off. He grinned, "That'll shake their lunch and give 'em something to talk about."

The general looked at his watch and stood up. "I've got a meeting in two minutes. You leaving tomorrow, Truck."

"I aimed to, General," Truck told him.

"Let's have supper at my house tonight," suggested Sullivan. "My wife still likes to have you around. She calls you the last of a breed. She's always favored the rough troopers over that bunch who hangs around Washington and the Pentagon."

"Well, Lefty, I always figured that lady was the best half of the family," Truck told him.

Sullivan laughed. He thought highly of the lady he was married to, and anyone who liked her as well had to be good people.

He looked at Dan, "Why don't you and your bride come also?"

"We'll be there," replied Dan.

"After we eat, we can go in the back room and talk about the next mission," said Sullivan. He put his empty cup down.

"I've got an idea what I want to do," said Truck.

"Spit it all out tonight. We'll mull it over and then talk to you about it," said Sullivan.

"Good. I'm on my way out to California to see Linn. If you've made up your mind in a few days, call me. If not, I'm going back to the Philippines. Me and the crew have some tactics we want to work out," Truck told him.

"That's a deal," the general said, dismissing them with a wave of his hand.

Truck and Dan left the building and walked back to Dan's office.

"See you tonight," Dan said, and went into the building.

Truck stood, waiting at the San Francisco Airport for his next flight south to see Linn. It was going to be good to see his only daughter. She was the thing he missed most when running these missions all over the world.

General Wallace would not commit himself on the team's next mission. Truck wanted to go to Laos and try rescuing American POWs that were being held in camps in the Sam Neua area. The Lao freedom fighters were inside Laos fighting the Pathet Lao Communists and Vietnamese at the present time. Now was the time to pull an operation. Such an operation would settle once and for all the matter about there being American POWs in Laos. Then the question of prisoners in Vietnam would be the only one left. Truck hoped someone would move on this quickly. It was long overdue. Like since 1973.

The music paused for a newscast to come on over the intercom system. The voice said that a special force of the Philippines' antiterrorist unit had located where Ybarra and his children were being held. By using tactics that the Filipinos had perfected, they had entered the hideout where the Ybarras were being held by a group of Communist terrorists under the leadership of a man called Aguerrido. His real name was Juan Serna and he was suspected of being one of the commanders of the Communist terrorist groups called "sparrows."

In the night attack upon the hideout, Aguerrido was killed. Ybarra and his children were released. Ybarra and his two daughters were hospitalized from the brutal treatment and torture they received while held by the sparrows. The son of Ybarra, it was reported, had gone into a catatonic state from seeing his sisters brutalized and gang-raped day after day by their captors. The girls' ages were six and seven.

The rest of the newscast was about the slow disbandment of the NPA as a military force and of the slowly diminishing ranks of the CPP.

Truck smiled. He and his team had been part of the reason for that.

He stopped off at a bar in the airport and bought a Jack Daniel's. He raised his glass to toast his friend Nick and the other Americans who had been assassinated by Communist sparrow terrorist teams. He raised his glass in a second toast to Chuck Taylor, who would soon retire as a captain. He raised his glass in a last toast in honor of the team and the Philippine military.